CURSED

MORWITCH SERIES
BOOK THREE

JENNIFER REDMILE

COVER DESIGN: Brendan McGaw

CHAPTER ONE

Ellie

*E*llie sighed with pleasure as she took her first sip of coffee. Savouring the delicious taste and the delectable aroma, she sipped slowly, knowing it was the only one she'd be allowed until tomorrow. Okay, so maybe she was guilty of worshipping the coffee like some kind of idol. But when your usual coffee intake was reduced to one measly cup a day just because you were pregnant, something had to give.

As if to remind her of the importance of the precious cargo inside her, a series of kicks almost made her spill the other precious cargo she currently held in her hands.

Seriously girls? Is it too much to ask that I have ten uninterrupted minutes out of my entire day? She smiled as the kicking immediately stopped.

She didn't mean to be such a cranky cow, but the pregnancy hormones seemed to get more out of control every day. But then, maybe the fact that she was carrying twins meant all the usual symptoms were doubled.

Yep, the Stars, in all their wisdom, had decided to gift them with twins. Although Ellie had a few more appropriate words than *gift* to describe carrying two babies around twenty-four-seven. She was already the size of a beached whale—well, in her opinion, anyway—and felt like she was growing bigger every minute.

Determined to snap herself out of her current foul mood, she gazed out the window of her reading room in Raythawn Castle. Even after two years of living in the Dragon Realm, she was still in awe of the now-familiar sight of a dragon or two flying by. Well, considering she was pregnant to a dragon shifter and carrying his babies, she'd *want* to be used to the sight.

Just thinking about Jayce, her gorgeous dragon shifter husband, soul mate and familiar all wrapped up in one incredibly perfect package, her mood lifted immediately. Not that he could have been described as the perfect package when they'd first met. In fact, she'd thought he was an arrogant, self-centred arsehole she'd wanted to punch in the face and kick to the kerb.

But the relationship they'd developed while running for their lives had become so much more than just a bond between a witch and her familiar. She still thanked the Stars every morning when she opened her eyes for bringing him into her life. The love they shared was far beyond anything she could have imagined possible.

She was snapped out of her thoughts by the sound of Jayce's smooth, sexy voice entering her head.

Hey baby, how are you doing up there? Do you need anything?

Speak of the devil! Ellie loved that their bond as witch and familiar granted them a telepathic link, a rare gift even among other bonded pairs. But she hoped he hadn't heard her indulging in her own personal pity party. She'd thought he was still at work, and understood his need to shut down the connection while ensuring the smooth running of the Dragon Realm.

Yes, as a matter of fact, I do need something, but only because you offered. I would so love it if you could carry these two babies around for a while. I mean, I love them, but my body just wants a break. So whadya think? Pleeeaasse... just for an hour or so? Surely there is some spell that can make it possible...

She immediately felt guilty for complaining about her situation. Poor Jayce never stopped running around trying to keep everyone happy. The last thing he needed was her whining too. She really needed to get these pregnancy hormones under control. She sounded like a spoiled princess.

As always, Jayce teleported to her side at the first sign of her unhappiness. Which, of course, made her feel even more like a spoiled brat.

"Hey beautiful girl," Jayce said, kneeling down in front of her chair and taking both her hands in his. "I *so* wish I could do this for you. But just think, as soon as they're born, there'll be so many people offering to carry them around you'll be demanding they give them back."

She smiled at the evidence of how well he knew her. That sounded exactly like something she would do. Her man's honey-gold eyes shone with love, and Ellie knew he would always do everything in his power to make her and their babies' lives better. She just needed to get over the whole *man-carrying-the-baby-during-pregnancy* thing being outside said power.

As was the norm in everything Jayce and Ellie did, no one knew what to expect from a half-mortal, half-witch pregnant with half-dragon and half-morwitch twins. Sure, she'd spoken to Iridia, Jayce's mum, about the whole *carrying-and-birthing-a-baby-dragon-shifter* thing. But Iridia was a dragon shifter herself, so Ellie had no idea how much of what the older dragon told her would apply in her case.

Iridia *had* assured her that dragon babies were usually about the same size and gestational period as mortal babies. But twin part dragon shifters who would likely carry magic? Nope... no records of *that* ever happening before existed. *Typical!*

But then, since when did any of the previously-unheard-of things Ellie and Jayce were capable of doing make sense? The crazy abilities they shared due to their bond *almost* explained why the bond had been outlawed in the first place.

Wait... I take that back. Nothing *explained or justified why the councils had sentenced us to death for an accidental bond being created between two totally unaware teenagers!*

Ellie sighed—something she seemed to be doing a lot lately—telling herself to get over being a grumpy cow and just enjoy the rare time alone with Jayce. Except for when they were in bed, someone always seemed to need Jayce for something. As head of the Dragon Council, it seemed that no one could make a move without running it by him first.

Not that Jayce encouraged this behaviour; they just all worshipped the ground he walked on and never wanted to do anything that might upset him. Yeah, well, maybe Ellie could relate to feeling like that, but *she* was *allowed* to monopolise him. *They* all just needed to grow some balls and do their jobs.

Feeling a couple of powerful kicks, Ellie pulled Jayce's hands against her ginormous stomach, sharing a goofy grin as they felt their two girls kicking and rolling as if playing a game together. Ellie and Jayce had learned they were having twin girls at their twelve-week scan. Although everyone had assured her it wasn't necessary, Ellie had decided she wanted to see an obstetrician. Having been raised by her aunts Emelda and Serena in the mortal realm for the first eighteen years of her life, she still preferred to embrace *some* mortal practices over those of her other heritage.

And, of course, Jayce had known better than to argue, sensible husband that he was.

"I still can't believe this is all real. I can remember more than a few times wondering if we'd survive long enough to *ever* contemplate having a normal future."

Jayce's eyes softened, a smile tugging at his lips. "I know, baby. And now, here we are, living the dream. Happily married and expecting not one but two witchling, dragonling babies," he mused, squeezing her hand with his own. "Hey, maybe we should try to come up with a name for their mixed heritage. I mean, you're a Morwitch. How do we incorporate the word dragon into that somehow?"

"Mordragwitch?"

"Widramor?"

"Dramorwitch?"

They both started to laugh as the suggestions became more ridiculous. Until Ellie eventually had to either call a halt or wet herself. She gratefully accepted Jayce's help getting out of her chair—marveling at how much easier it was with help—and quickly headed to the bathroom for the umpteenth time that day—yet another one of the joys of pregnancy.

Seriously? Why did women choose *to go back and do this over and over again? Maybe their brains just deleted all the bad stuff until it was too late to change their mind.*

The minute she stepped out of the bathroom Jayce pulled her into his arms. "So… whatever racemash name they end up with, I'm sure our baby girls will be every bit as fierce and… gorgeous as their mother."

"Oooh, I was sure you were going to throw the *stubborn* word in there. Ever the diplomat, my darling," Ellie teased.

"I think you can put *that* down to learned behaviour," Jayce replied with a cheeky grin. Ellie stepped out of Jayce's arms and was heading back to her recliner when she felt an unfamiliar energy begin coursing through her. It was as if an alien had invaded her body and was racing from cell to cell. She turned back to tell Jayce what was happening when she caught sight of her hands, and froze in horror.

Stars almighty, either I'm suffering from hallucinations or my hands are glowing.

"Jayce? Can you see this? Are my hands really—"

Her words were cut off when the foreign energy seemed to burst from her fingertips, sending waves of what had to be magic pulsing outward. Ellie would have fallen if Jayce hadn't pulled her back into his arms and held her against him. They both stared in horror at the smouldering burn mark marring the wall on the other side of the room.

"Wh…what the hell is going on?" Ellie felt like she was losing her mind, along with control of her body and her magic. "Since when does my magic have a mind of its own?"

"So, you didn't…?" Jayce asked carefully.

"Nope. I was just a passenger. Apparently, my magic is happy to drive itself now."

"O-kaaay, so maybe it might be an idea to have a chat with your mother about magical pregnancies, and see if this kind of thing is normal or just another side effect of our bond. But seriously, sweetheart, are *you* okay?" Jayce asked, holding her close.

"Yeah, I'm fine. Just a bit freaked out. "Wait… what about the babies? Oh, Stars, Jayce. What if—"

"Stop stressing, my love," Jayce said against her ear. "I'm sure they'd be letting us know if something was wrong. Besides, would it really surprise you to learn that *they* might have been behind the whole thing? You know, kinda stretching their magic like other babies stretch their limbs." As if they'd heard what Jayce said, two strong kicks pushed against the inside of Ellie's belly.

They both chuckled, and Ellie's panic faded away. Okay, so maybe Jayce was right, and the babies had just been testing their strength. But, if so, she really hoped *that* wouldn't be a habit they repeated often.

Ellie's hand rubbed against her swollen belly. She was suddenly exhausted from whatever had caused the rogue magic episode. Jayce's larger hand moved to cover hers, their fingers intertwining. He kissed her forehead, and she sighed in contented bliss.

"Oh, I keep forgetting to tell you, I have another scan due this week. So, the aunts have been asking me to come for a longer visit instead of just popping in after my appointments. What do you think about me spending a couple of days in the Mortal Realm with them?"

Jayce frowned, his hands tensing where she held them against her stomach. "You know I hate it when we're apart. And there's no way I can get away this week for more than an hour or so for the scan. Maybe it would be better if we arranged it for after next month's scan. That way I can make sure I'm free for a couple of days."

Ellie tried not to let her disappointment show, but Jayce's reaction told her how badly she'd failed at *that.* "Fine. I suppose I can put it off until next month. Even if the aunts have already been baking for days so they could spoil me with all my favourites."

She tried to hold back the tears welling in her eyes. *For Star's sake!* Since being pregnant, her brain had apparently lost all control over her tear ducts, which now leaked at random. *Damned hormones!*

Jayce wrapped his arms as far around her as he could reach and placed a tender kiss on her forehead. Ellie sighed and wished they could hug like they used to. She couldn't wait until her oversized belly was gone, and she could go back to feeling completely enveloped in Jayce's strong arms.

CHAPTER TWO

Jayce

At the sight of the tears welling in Ellie's eyes, Jayce reached an arm down behind Ellie's knees and lifted her into his arms. Her contented sigh told him how much she'd needed some pampering, and he wanted to kick his own butt for neglecting her needs for way too long.

Kissing her forehead again, he moved to the over-sized lounge, a recent addition to what he called Ellie's 'woman cave'. He sat and smiled as Ellie practically wrapped herself around him.

He glanced at his watch and sighed, knowing he was due in an important meeting in fifteen minutes. Still, after seeing Ellie in this emotionally wrung-out state, he knew it was way past time to reassess his priorities.

Her deep breathing told him she'd nodded off, and he decided he could put off leaving for the meeting for an extra ten minutes. Sighing in contentment at the feel of Ellie snuggled against him, he allowed his mind to meander down memory lane.

He'd enjoyed helping restore the Dragon Realm to its former glory for the past two years. There had been a gargantuan mess to clean up, reassessing and reversing the proclamations responsible for banishing innocent dragons from the realm due to his step-father Thomas' greed and insatiable quest for power.

He shuddered as thoughts of what Thomas had tried to do slipped through the walls he'd erected around the memories of that time. Thank the Stars the monster was dead, even if it had to be at Jayce's own hands.

He looked down at Ellie's beautiful face nestled against his chest and promised himself to make the time to sit with her like this more often. Then, pushing all the memories back into their box, he focused on the present.

It was time to make some changes in the Dragon Council hierarchy and restore his own family to the forefront. He was sick of the other councilors' constant need for validation, resulting in their inability to make decisions without his approval. So, after today's meeting, there would be some long-overdue changes to the chain of command. Delegation would be his new friend.

He was surprised by the surge of relief flooding his body at the thought of reducing his workload. He hadn't been aware of how heavy the burden of splitting his time between work responsibilities and his family had become. Ellie and his girls were the most important things in his life, and it was way past time he proved it.

He felt Ellie begin to stir against him, and decided it was time to share his thoughts with her. Usually, she'd have been able to listen to his thoughts through their link, but one of them sleeping had always provided a reprieve from that sometimes-intrusive ability.

"Oops… did I really nod off? Why didn't you wake me?" Ellie's voice held that sexy huskiness it always did when she first woke up. It made him want to cancel the damn meeting and just stay right where he was. *Nope… not gonna happen.*

"Why would I?" Jayce replied with a cheeky smile. "You know how much I love watching you sleep. Besides, it gave me some time to think. And before you throw in some smart-arse comment, just listen, okay?"

"Fine. But it better be good news," Ellie huffed.

"Okay… how about this? I have a Council meeting I need to attend soon, after which I intend to implement some significant changes to the Dragon Council officers' duties. This means I'll be delegating a lot of the decision-making responsibilities and refusing to be *the buck-stops-here* person for every bloody move they make. Then I'll finally be able to spend more time with you and the girls."

Ellie opened her mouth to speak, but Jayce held up a hand. If he was really serious about trying to make her happy, he needed to suck up his earlier worries about the visit to the aunts as well.

"*And…* if you really want to do this overnight visit with the aunts this week, I suppose I can live with it. I won't be able to stay overnight with you, but at least I'll be there for the ultrasound. After that, I'll get you settled at the aunts' and be back to pick you up Wednesday afternoon. But this will be the *only* time we're apart for the foreseeable future. How does that sound?"

"*Yess!*" Ellie struggled to do the fist pump from where she was tucked in beside him, and he chuckled as she started to kiss every inch of his face. "Thank you —*kiss.* Thank you—*kiss.* Thank you—*kiss.*"

"I'm just glad I can do something to make you happy again. I've been so busy sorting out other people's crap that I let 'us' slip from where we belong in the big picture, which I'm sure you'd agree should always be at the forefront. So, if we want this new *Ellie-and-my-girls-must-always-come-first* plan happening sooner rather than later, I'll need to get going. When is your appointment?"

"Ummm… tomorrow at 10 am, I think. I'll check in a minute. This whole *baby-brain-memory-loss* thing is getting worse." She groaned at the effort of trying to manoeuvre herself out of Jayce's lap and off the lounge. Unable to hold back the laugh at the look of deep concentration on her face, Jayce stood up with her still in his arms before letting her legs drop to the ground.

"Damnit Elle, if this is how hard it is to function at six months, how the hell are you gonna cope when you get even bigger?"

Ellie growled—*yep, it had definitely been a growl*—and slapped his arm. "Don't even think about me getting any bigger than this. These girls do *not* need to get any bigger than they are right now, thank you very much. They can spend the next three months developing whatever body parts they're supposed to. But getting bigger while still inside me is not an option."

Jayce threw back his head and roared with laughter. He bent down until his mouth was next to Ellie's tummy and dropped his voice to a whisper. "Did you hear that, girls? I would strongly advise you to do as your mama says because it's not pretty when you cross her. Trust me, I know from experience."

He kissed her belly where his daughters currently resided and grinned at his wife. "Okay, they've been warned."

"Well, I certainly hope their ears are fully developed and in complete working order. Now, you need to get to your meeting, and I need to start packing."

"Packing? You're only going for one night."

"I can't believe you've forgotten what I told you

after I fetched our clothes that first time. A woman needs to have choices available at all times."

Learning to magically 'fetch' whatever she needed had been the first ability Ellie's mother had taught her. As long as she could envisage in her mind where something was, she could just hold out her hand and it would appear. While on the run, they'd discovered she could also 'fetch' something she'd never seen as long as Jayce could see it. Yet another one of those previously unheard of things they could do thanks to their weird bond.

Jayce chuckled, and then sighed in contentment. This was how he wanted his life to be all the time. Sitting with Ellie wrapped in his arms with no worries or thoughts of the worlds around them.

"You have no idea how much I love you, my beautiful witchy-girl. I didn't realise at the time, but until we met, I was just surviving. Now... I have everything." Then he kissed her. And, as always, life was perfect.

Ellie

LESS THAN AN HOUR LATER, Ellie was struggling to hide her smile at the sight of her mother attempting to hold back her frustration. She kept expecting the older witch to stamp her foot and burst into tears. "I don't understand why I can't just go with you, sweetheart. You know I'd love to spend some time with the aunts too. And then I'd be there if you need me. What if something—"

Ellie held up her hand and huffed. "Wait, wait, wait… Before you say something you can't take back. You seem to have forgotten I'm a very accomplished and self-sufficient witch too. If anything happens, I can still just teleport home, even if I am pregnant."

"Yes, darling, I'm quite aware of all that. But you won't even be able to message Jayce through the bond while you're in separate realms. What if—"

"Mum. You need to stop. I'll be fine. I want to do this... alone. I do not need to be watched twenty-four-seven, which is exactly how I feel lately. You all seem to have forgotten that I helped save the Mortal Realm a couple of years ago and can actually look after myself. I am far from being a damsel-in-distress. Never have been and never will be."

"But now there are two babies—"

"Who are both perfectly happy right where they are. And seeing no one else can carry them around at the moment, I guess I'll just have to be responsible for all three of us. Now, do you plan to help me pack, or was the offer just a ruse to try and convince me to let you come to the Mortal Realm to see the aunts with me?"

Her mother managed to look slightly shamefaced,

and Ellie laughed. "Okay, you're forgiven. And seeing I can fetch what I need and send it to the suitcase, the helping me part is a bit redundant anyway, don't you think?"

"Fine," the older woman huffed. "I'll just go do something useful then and make us a cup of tea."

"That sounds awesome. Thanks, Mum," Ellie called as her mother practically stomped from the room.

Ellie had been sitting on her bed while arguing with her mother, and she smiled as she allowed her head to fall backwards onto the pillow. She got that her poor mum had been robbed of almost eighteen years of her daughter's life, all because her family and the Witch Council had been racist pigs over Ellie's half-mortal status.

Ellie smiled as she remembered the outrage on the faces of some of the Witch Council's members when she'd stood before them and told them to get over themselves. Needless to say, the whole inter-racial crap had been rectified soon after.

The problem was that her mum, trying to make up for lost time, had become a tad over-protective. At least, she *tried* to be. The older witch had quickly learned that her own stubborn nature was no match for her daughter's. Even Jayce was always saying that her stubborn pride made her a total pain in the arse at times. But hey, he'd also told her on equally as many occasions that he loved her, warts and all.

Deciding that two arguments in the same day had

just about wiped out her previous desire for a suitcase-packing-extravaganza, she closed her eyes and snuggled down against her body pillow. She'd just close them for a minute and then get on with it, which were her last thoughts as she drifted off to sleep… again.

CHAPTER THREE

Jayce

Having finished with the dreaded Council meeting, Jayce stood in the doorway of the bedroom he and Ellie shared, and contentment flooded his veins. Watching Ellie sleep had long been one of his favourite pastimes, and since she'd become pregnant the opportunities had multiplied. Out of the blue, a memory of a conversation they'd had on the way to saving the Tree of Life popped into his head.

"Damn, I love watching you sleep. One day, when this is all over, I'm gonna spend an entire day doing it."

Ellie chuckled. "What makes you think I'd want to sleep all day so you could watch me?"

Jayce's smouldering eyes glowed. "Guess I'll have to make sure you're too exhausted to argue with me for once. I can think of a few ways I could guarantee that."

He smiled at the memory. He'd known Ellie was his everything from the beginning, and soon they would have two new additions to their perfect world.

Although, to be honest, he'd never even thought of getting her pregnant with twins so he could spend more time watching her sleep.

Well, lucky you admitted it was not *one of the reasons I'm now pregnant with twins. Otherwise, you'd be searching for your balls right about now.*

Jayce burst out laughing at the sound of Ellie's voice in his head. *Exactly how long have you been awake, witchy woman?*

About as long as you've been standing there in the door-way, allowing your mind to shout things into my head.

Ellie's soft chuckle was like music to his ears. *I can't believe you still haven't learned your lesson about listening in to my random thoughts.*

Jayce smiled at the memory of Ellie's mortified expression when she'd inadvertently read some thoughts he'd been having about... let's just call them rather X rated activities.

Well, maybe those thoughts don't have the same effect on me as they used to. I'm not some timid little virgin any more...remember?

Jayce threw his head back and laughed. *I'm sorry sweetheart, but the word timid could never have been applied to you.*

Jayce climbed into the bed beside her, and they snuggled silently for a while. He relished the peace after the discord at the meeting he'd just left. As if she were reading his thoughts, Ellie broke the silence.

"So… did everything go alright at the meeting?"

Jayce tried not to tense up as he replayed the aftermath of the meeting. No one had been happy about his announcement. Still, he was confident that the changes would work once they all got their heads out of their arses. "Well… they weren't exactly agreeable, but they'll get over it… eventually."

"Maybe you should have just told them to stop acting like princesses and do their jobs."

Jayce could hear the suppressed laughter in her voice, and the stress melted away again. This was where he needed to be, and she was who he needed to be with. Maybe he should have used those exact words when he told the other Councillors to step up.

He couldn't hold back his chuckle when he spied the empty suitcase sitting on the floor beside the bed. "I see you changed your mind about needing to take a large choice of clothing to the aunts. Although I can't see taking nothing working very well either."

Ellie slapped his chest and giggled. "I just needed a quick nap before I got to the serious stuff," she said, and he could hear the cheeky lilt in her voice.

"Ohhh? I can't wait to hear what constitutes the *serious stuff!*"

"You're joking, right? I'd have thought that was just common sense. Making the wrong decision about what *not* to take can have serious repercussions. What if I forget to take something and I need it? I mean, we'll be in separate realms. I won't be able to just ask you to bring it over for me. I'd have to teleport all the way home and back again."

Before Jayce could say a word, she burst out laughing. "You should see the look on your face! I wish I had a camera on me. I love you so much." She spluttered the words through her laughter, and he couldn't help joining her.

When they were both finally back in control, he couldn't help stirring her up just a bit more. "Well, just let me know if need any help with your monumental task. No wait, I take that back. There's no way I'm helping just so you can blame me for whatever catastrophe occurs as a result of you leaving something important behind. Besides, I have something way more important for you to do before you get back to it. Like kissing your poor neglected husband."

CHAPTER FOUR

Ellie

"**W**ell, everything seems to be going well, Mrs Raythawn," the doctor conducting the ultrasound said with a smile. "The babies are both unusually large for twins, but that's a good thing, as identical twins can often be on the smaller side. But these two young ladies appear determined to consume as much nourishment as they can before they have to leave the womb."

"Oh, I don't think so. Because *these two young ladies* have been told they are not to get any bigger until they are *out* of said womb."

Ellie instantly regretted her words when she saw the look of horror on the doctor's face at her less-than-eloquent statement. Luckily, Jayce stepped in before the doctor could even think about reporting them for child abuse—if that was even possible while the babies were still in utero.

"Ummm... sorry. I don't think Ellie meant that to sound the way it did. We're just happy to know the girls are both healthy and thriving." He threw Ellie a *don't-you-dare-argue-with-me* look, and she just shrugged.

What, did this doctor seriously think I might try to deprive the babies of nourishment for my own benefit? How the hell could anyone *do that?*

All thoughts were erased as a stabbing pain shot through her belly. *What the hell was going on now?* The pain was similar to the old bad-feeling she used to get whenever something wasn't right.

"Elle, what's wrong, sweetheart? Are you okay? Is it the—"

Ellie bit her lip and shook her head. "I'm fine, baby. Just a muscle cramp or something. It's gone now," she lied, trying to push the pain down as she looked at the doctor. "Are we done yet? Because I really need to find a ladies' room."

The doctor patted her hand and looked at Jayce. "It's possible your wife is having Braxton hicks. They are usually mild cramps and nothing to worry about." He moved his eyes to Ellie and frowned. "But if they become regular, it might be best to make an appointment with your doctor. Twins tend to up the ante on the risk factors. Okay then, we're done for now.

There's a bathroom in the waiting room, and I'll see you next month."

Ellie bit back a moan, and Jayce picked her up and pulled her against his chest. *What the hell is going on, Elle?*

Not sure. Bad-feeling maybe? Please just get us out of here. Ellie moaned again and then sighed with relief when Jayce hurried out of the doctor's office, stepped into a nearby alley, and teleported them to the aunts' house.

"Hello, my sweet. We're so glad—" Ellie looked up from where her head had been resting on Jayce's shoulder to find Aunt Emelda standing frozen in the doorway as she took in the scene unfolding before her.

"What's happened? Ellie, you're white as a sheet," she said, recovering enough to cross the room and indicate the lounge where Jayce should deposit Ellie.

Jayce placed her gently where he'd been told, then stepped back and growled, interrupting any hope of Ellie answering her aunt. "I'm sorry, Elle, but I'm going to get your mum. She's always been the best at figuring out how to fix this. I'll be right back."

Jayce had vanished before Ellie could say a word, and she felt the tears burning behind her eyes. This was utter bullshit. She'd not had a feeling this bad since they'd disposed of Thomas Raythawn, and she'd hoped never to again.

"Ellie honey, can you—" The arrival of her mum and

Jayce cut off Emelda's words. Her mum was trying to hide the panic in her eyes and doing a terrible job of it.

"Mum? Sorry, but it's charades time again. You up for it?" Ellie asked, trying to lighten the tension in the room. Her mother had always been able to narrow down what event had triggered the onset of what they'd come to call her bad-feeling, and Ellie prayed she could do it again.

Her mum sat on the arm of Ellie's chair and swept the hair off her sweaty forehead. She turned toward Jayce and asked if he could remember what they'd been talking about when it came on.

"Sure do. It's a long story, but the gist of it is that Ellie was sick of having to carry the twins around all the time and wanted someone else to take over for a while. I asked her how she was going to cope when the babies got bigger, and she banned them from growing any more while in utero. Then, *I* stupidly warned the girls to listen to their mother."

"Anyway, the subject of the babies' birth weight came up at the ultrasound, and the doctor said the girls are already large for twins. To say the doctor was shocked when Ellie told him they wouldn't be getting any bigger would be an understatement. I'm pretty sure he thought we were somehow gonna cut off their food supply or something equally ridiculous."

Ellie cried out as another spasm rocketed through her, and her mother flinched. "Sounds to me like your babies are worried as much as the doctor was. They don't know that what's being discussed is impossible, so they're freaking out. You both need to tell them you're sorry and that nothing like that will happen."

Jayce raced over and knelt in front of Ellie, where Emelda had been sitting earlier. He placed his hands on Ellie's belly, and she saw the first tear run down his face. "Hey now, my beautiful baby girls. Daddy would never let any harm come to his precious angels. I am so sorry for worrying you with our silly words. Mummy is sorry, too."

Ellie felt the pain begin to melt away and sagged in relief. *Wow... talk about the power of words.* She swore she'd never say another word without considering how those words could affect someone else. She hadn't even realised Emelda had left until she spied the woman entering the room with the familiar overladen tray, the delicious smell wafting from something on the tray making her mouth water.

"Well, you're certainly looking better than when you arrived, my sweet. And it looks like those babies are doing well too. Serena won't be long. She'll be devastated when she discovers you arrived without her here to greet you."

Ellie just smiled, nodded and closed her eyes. She'd been so scared that the pain was an indication that something was physically wrong with her pregnancy. How could she have not considered that her babies would hear and understand everything that was going on outside the womb. Their DNA was loaded with magic, for Star's sake. Of course they were far more capable than anyone gave them credit for. Even *before* they were born.

I'm so sorry, my darlings. I had no idea that saying those things would hurt you. Daddy and I love you with everything we are and we can't wait to meet you.

She felt a thumb sweep under one eye and then the other, and then Jayce was scooping her up—again—off the lounge and stealing her seat, keeping her in his arms as she snuggled into him. As always, Ellie felt the infusion of strength she'd grown to expect from Jayce as he held her.

"Everything is fine, beautiful girl. The whole thing was just a total misunderstanding. But we definitely learned one thing from this. Our girls are very aware of what's going on outside their little bubble."

Ellie just nodded and snuggled in closer. She knew this wasn't the time to tell Jayce that the bad feeling hadn't gone away completely, just settled into a dull ache.

Jayce

SOMETIMES, Jayce wished Ellie could be a *little* bit less stubborn. This was definitely one of those times. After dealing with Ellie's bad-feeling, they'd all settled down to enjoy a mouth-wateringly good lunch provided by the aunts. Ellie seemed to be back to her old self, and he was hoping to convince her to go home with him today. He just wanted—*no, needed*—her close.

With a full stomach and no immediate worries, Jayce sat in perfect contentment with his eyes closed and his head resting against the back of the lounge. He was just starting to nod off when Ellie gasped and wriggled against him.

"Stars Jayce, what are you still doing here? Didn't you have a really important Council meeting today?"

"Yeah, don't worry; I asked Yvette to let them know the meeting would be later this afternoon." He tried not to laugh at the memory of Yvette practically throwing a tantrum before agreeing to leave. Only after she was sure Ellie was okay did she huff and then vanish.

"Well then, you'd better get going," Ellie said.

"Ummm… so about that. I was thinking that maybe after everything that's happened today, you might—"

"Don't you dare finish that sentence! I thought we already had this argument, and you agreed I could stay."

"But that was before—"

"Jayce, I'm fine. The bad thing already happened, so it's not like anything else is going to—"

"Damnit Elle, can I at least finish a sentence?" Jayce

growled, his patience evaporating at the speed of light. "What if something else happens? I won't be here to go for help. Okay, so you might still be able to teleport under normal circumstances, but what if you slipped and fell and ended up unconscious? We both know you wouldn't be capable of teleporting. Did you even consider that?"

"Jayce... I really need this. Please? There must be some way I could still stay without you turning into a stressed mess."

Jayce sighed and gave up. He knew better than anyone that continuing to argue with Ellie once she'd dug her heels in was pointless

"Okay, I give up. But if anything happens—" Jayce was interrupted by Ellie's squeal of excitement as she threw her arms around his neck and kissed him. And, as always, the kiss drove all other thoughts from his head.

When he finally had his thoughts together enough to stand up to leave for the meeting, Jayce tried to ignore the sense of unease causing his stomach to twist. He couldn't shake the thought that bad things happened when they were apart. But that had been while they were running for their lives and battling Thomas' tyranny. This was just an overnight stay with the aunts—totally different scenarios.

"*Holy Shining Stars Jayce!* I just thought of a way I can contact you." She removed the bracelet he'd given her for their first wedding anniversary from her wrist, reached for his hand and placed it on his palm. Then she wrapped his fingers around it and smiled. "I don't know why some magic is possible when we're in different realms and some isn't, but we've always been able to fetch something, even between realms. So, as long as you still have this, then you'll know I'm fine."

Jayce felt as though the weight of the world had been lifted off his shoulders. His beautiful girl was a genius! He leaned back down to where she sat on the lounge and kissed her forehead. "Thank you, sweetheart. Like I've said many times, beautiful *and* brilliant. I'm a lucky man."

Ellie's chuckle was warm and loving. "Well then, lucky man, time to get your butt into gear and go solve the problems of the worlds. Well, the dragon world, at least."

Jayce straightened back up, called out a goodbye to the aunts in the kitchen, blew her a kiss and mouthed *I love you*. Then, the floor fell away beneath him, and he was on his way back to the Dragon Realm.

CHAPTER FIVE

Valerius

alerius Thornweaver had been overjoyed when he'd first received the news that Thomas Raythawn, the spawn-of-the-devil dragon shifter and head of the Dragon Council, was finally dead. Thomas was the monster who had been responsible for both of Valerius' parents being burned to death. It didn't matter that his parents had merely been in the wrong place at the wrong time; Thomas Raythawn was the one who'd ordered the incineration of the building where they were staying.

Then, to add further insult to injury, Valerius, out of his mind with grief, had killed another fae and been banished from the Fae Realm to live out his existence in the Mortal Realm. So, Thomas had been responsible for yet another injustice forced upon the previously mild-mannered young fae.

His scars ran deep, festering and inflaming his need for revenge. But over the years, that unfulfilled revenge had become tainted until he only knew that no dragon should be free of his vengeance. So, he had spent the years languishing in the Mortal Realm, seeking out and destroying any dragons unlucky enough to cross his path.

But the news of Thomas Raythawn's death had been almost two years ago, and this latest news he'd received had his insatiable desire for revenge raising its ugly head again. He'd thought hearing of Thomas' death had assuaged the feeling, but knowing he hadn't been the one responsible for the old dragon's death had dimmed some of the pleasure he'd expected to feel. But now... he'd been granted a second chance.

He paced the floor of his tiny studio apartment, his excitement building to an all-new high. Thomas had a son, who was married with twins on the way. Two more devil's spawn abominations to be spewed into the worlds. How could anything produced by Thomas' DNA not be a blight on the worlds?

After much consideration of the matter, he'd decided that it was his *personal responsibility* to ensure that the evil creatures never took their first breath. He was convinced that these actions would finally end the compulsion for revenge that had consumed his every waking moment.

It had taken him months to procure the curse that would end the creatures' existence while still in utero, and no one would ever know their stillbirth was anything more than a natural occurrence. The curse itself was ingenious. It would convince the mother's brain to slowly restrict the nutrients being sent to the babies, and they'd be dead before she reached full term.

Now, the only thing left to do to bring his plan to fruition was to find an opportunity to place the curse on the unsuspecting mother. He had kept a close eye on his intended victim and knew she often visited the Mortal Realm. But she was never without Thomas' spawn, the dragon shifter Jayce Raythawn. This meant that Valerius was running out of time for the curse to be effective.

According to his calculations, the happy couple had come to the Mortal Realm every month for the last four months, and today was the day they were due to visit again. He knew they usually visited some relatives or friends in a house across the road from the lake, so he would don the harmless, friendly old man persona and hang out in the park. All he had to do was touch the woman's bare flesh, and the curse would be activated.

As he wove the glamour to adopt his often-used persona, he sang a little ditty his mother used to sing to him as a child.

Mama, this is for you and Da. I'm sorry it's taken so long.

Smiling and throwing a kiss at the photo of his dead parents, he pulled his old hat off the rack, grabbed some stale bread to feed the ducks, and headed out for a lovely day at the park.

Ellie

SITTING on the porch swing on the front verandah of her childhood home, Ellie smiled at the hyperactivity in which the twins were currently engaged. It was always like this when their father left to go anywhere. Rubbing her belly in a circular motion with both hands, she could have sworn the kicking moved to the spot directly under where she rubbed.

Hey, you pair, Daddy won't be gone long. He'll be back in the morning to get us, so stop stressing and taking it out on me.

The kicking stopped immediately, and Ellie sagged against the back of the swing. Today had been one of her most challenging days in over two years. She was still concerned about the dull ache that seemed to have settled into her bones. She hoped it was just the result of tiredness due to the pregnancy and nothing more sinister.

She looked longingly over at the park, the brilliant sunshine reflecting off the lake, making it appear to glow. She smiled at the sight of an old man breaking up bits of bread and throwing them to the ducks. Stars, she'd love to be doing something like that. She used to—

Wait, why couldn't she do it right now? She could just grab some stale bread from the kitchen and waddle over the road to join the old man. It wasn't like she was really leaving the house. She'd always considered the park and the lake an extension of the aunts' front yard. Besides, she'd be back here sitting on the swing in five minutes, and no one would even know she'd left. She struggled to her feet and went to the kitchen to get some bread, brimming with excitement at her planned adventure.

Valerius

VALERIUS CURSED under his breath as he watched the pregnant woman climb off the swing and head inside. He'd been waiting for the dragon spawn husband, who seemed determined never to let her out of his sight, to join her on the swing. But no, she'd sat there alone and then gone back inside. Damnit, he needed to think of a way to touch her with the cursed object as soon as possible. She was obviously very pregnant, and she'd be going back to the dragon realm any minute. Hey, she might have gone inside to do just that.

And then it happened. Valerius held his breath as he watched his intended victim walk back out the front door, down the steps from the verandah, open the small gate, and head across the road toward the park. But the best part? She was alone! He watched the front door, expecting the dragon spawn to come running out the door after her, but no—no one came out the door, and she had already crossed the road and looked to be headed for the lake. Then he spotted the small container in her hands and almost laughed out loud as he realised she was coming to feed the ducks with what she perceived as the nice old man.

Valerius wanted to hoot with delight at his incredible luck. She was actually coming to him, and all he had to do was accidentally brush against her flesh for the curse to take effect. Hell's bells and highwater, this would be as easy as taking candy from a baby.

He smiled as she walked up beside him. "Well, hello there, mum-to-be. And pretty soon, by the looks of things."

The woman blushed and rubbed her belly self-consciously. "Actually, I'm only six months, but I'm having twins, so..." she shrugged and looked down at her belly.

Pity she'd tied herself to that dragon spawn. She was pretty and seemed sweet, but she had made her choice, and now she'd suffer the consequences. Opening the small container, she pulled out a few pieces of bread and threw them to the waiting ducks. Her face lit up with joy at the sight of them squabbling over the tiny morsel.

Stop looking at her and get the job done. Think of what she's carrying inside her, you stupid old goat. Valerius looked back to find her fishing the last of her offerings from the bottom of the container and knew he'd have to move fast. She wouldn't be there much longer.

Valerius made a show of trying to pull the last piece of bread out of the bottom of the bag he'd brought, fumbling the bag and aiming it to land close to her feet. "Oh, I'm so sorry, luv. Did it hit you? Bloody doddering old fool I am."

She smiled and shook her head, reaching down to grab the bag as he did the same. When their hands brushed against each other, he knew it was done. The cursed object had touched her hand, and it had begun.

Wanting to cheer and bounce around with delight, Valerius instead dragged the last piece of bread out, threw it to the ducks, and said his goodbyes, scurrying away as if the hounds of hell were on his tail. In fact, he practically ran all the way to his apartment, excitement and pride racing through his veins.

He'd done it! Valerius Thornweaver had single-handedly saved the worlds from certain doom. The yet-to-be-born devil spawn would not live long enough to take their first breath, and the devastation they'd have caused had been circumvented thanks to his diligence and personal quest for justice.

CHAPTER SIX

Ellie

Ellie threw the last of her bread to the ducks and turned to head back to the house. The dull ache she'd thought almost gone was back with a vengeance. Not to mention the onset of a headache that was starting to feel more like a migraine. Wait... how long had it been since she'd felt the babies move? She couldn't remember. *What in all the realms was going on?*

By the time she'd reached the front door, her entire body felt ready to give out. She stepped inside and practically crawled up the stairs to her room, hoping the pain would ease if she lay down for a while. After the whole fight with Jayce over going home early, her pride wouldn't allow her to give him the satisfaction of being proven right.

Wait... what if this bad feeling had something to do with Jayce? What if he was hurt or in trouble? She sucked in a long slow breath. No, her mother would have come for her if anything like that was wrong.

Ellie's biggest concern was the pounding in her head. It had never been a part of her bad-feelings before. Usually, the pain was only in her stomach.

Yeah, great. Apparently, the bad-feelings had decided to morph into something even more debilitating than they already had been. Yet another side effect of being pregnant? Probably.

Ellie groaned as her head hit the deliciously soft, fluffy pillow on her bed, and she was asleep before she'd even kicked off her shoes.

"Ellie darling, dinner's ready. You've been asleep all afternoon. Are you feeling okay?" Ellie opened her eyes to find Aunt Serena bending over her bed with her hands hovering above Ellie's forehead. If she were honest, Ellie felt how she imagined someone who'd been flattened by a dragon would feel. But she decided not to share how bad she felt with her always a worry-wart aunt.

"Yeah, yeah, I'm fine. I must have been more wiped out than I realised. I think I kinda passed out," Ellie explained as she yawned while trying to sit up in the bed.

"You certainly did, honey," Serena chuckled while helping Ellie sit up. "You didn't even take your shoes off."

Ellie blushed when she noticed the dirty marks on the quilt. "Oops… sorry. I'll fix—"

"Oh, pfft. You'll do no such thing. Emelda and I don't exactly have busy schedules. I'm sure we'll have time to fix one old quilt."

"You and Emelda must be so sick of cleaning up my messes by now. Who'd have thought you'd still be doing it even after I've grown up and left home? Sorry," Ellie shook her head, disgusted with herself for being so helpless. Where was the woman who could take down evil masterminds when she needed her? Oh yeah, *that* Ellie had left the building the minute she found out *this* Ellie was pregnant. *Typical.*

The thought of standing up to head downstairs for dinner made her aching head spin and her stomach heave. But she pushed past the discomfort and swung her legs to the ground. Which is when her entire body seemed to go haywire. The babies started to kick furiously, and her entire world lurched as she reached out for someone or something to break her fall. Knowing that there was a serious problem, she held out her shaking hand and fetched her bracelet, breathing a sigh of relief at the knowledge that Jayce would be there soon.

Jayce

THE MEETING SEEMED to go on forever, and Jayce had spent the entire time with his hand wrapped around the bracelet in his pocket. Just knowing he had a link to Ellie was the only thing keeping him from losing his mind. He'd always hated them being apart, but now, with the babies in the mix, his stomach was twisted into knots. He'd constantly berated Ellie whenever she started with the what-ifs, but right then, his mind was ready to explode as they seemed to multiply.

As soon as the meeting ended, Jayce practically ran from the meeting room, ignoring any and all of the enquiring looks and questions thrown at him. Eager to spread his wings and get home for dinner, he stepped out onto the cobbled grounds around the Council chambers and launched himself into the sky. As always, he was grateful that dragon shifters returned to the clothes they'd been wearing before they shifted. Most other shifters spent half their lives running around naked. *Yeah, no thanks.*

Jayce had been flying for less than five minutes when his head began to throb with a dull ache. Since pain in his dragon form only ever came from battle injuries, he knew something else must be wrong. *Ellie!* Fear and dread gripped him as he sped towards home.

After landing in the castle courtyard, Jayce shifted and then shoved his hand into his pocket. The bracelet was gone. Stars, how long had it been since he'd checked it? He raced in the front door and called for Yvette, somehow knowing they'd need the witch's support.

"I'm here, Jayce. What's wrong?" Yvette asked as she hurried down the stairs toward him.

"Ellie's in trouble. Don't ask me how I know. We need to go… *now.*"

Yvette paled and was gone before he could even blink. Jayce followed a heartbeat later.

Jayce fought down the panic rising in his throat when he found Ellie pale and shaking on the floor of her old room. *What the hell had happened in the few hours she'd been alone?* He dropped to the floor and pulled her into his arms.

"What is it, beautiful? What can I do to help?" Ellie looked up into his eyes and started to sob. Jayce pulled her into his lap and wrapped her up tight, immediately becoming aware of the incessant kicking coming from Ellie's belly.

Hey there, angel babies, Daddy's here. I think you might need to settle down a bit because Mummy's not well and needs some rest. He felt the kicking stop immediately, and Ellie relaxed in his arms. *Thank the stars for that, at least.* As Ellie's sobs turned into hiccups and gasps, he lifted her chin and looked into her panic-filled eyes.

"Can you tell me yet?" Jayce asked softly.

I don't know what happened. I was on the swing on the verandah watching this old guy feed the ducks in the lake. At least she could speak coherently through their telepathic link. Jayce looked up at the aunts and Yvette, pointing between his and Ellie's heads. They all sighed in understanding and settled themselves while they waited for him to tell them what she'd said.

Okay, baby, then what happened?

She took a deep breath and looked directly into his eyes. *You need to not get angry with me, okay?*

Stars Elle... why would I be angry with you?

Well, I wanted to feed the ducks, too, so I did. Ellie held her breath as if expecting him to blow up, and Jayce couldn't help chuckling. She looked at him in shock. *But I promised I wouldn't go anywhere or leave the house alone.*

Oh, Elle. I know you've always considered the park just an extension of the aunts' yard. But I don't get what that has to do with why you're in this state?

Because that's where it all started, and I was too stubborn to tell anyone that the bad feeling hadn't completely gone away. It had just become more tolerable, like a dull ache in the background.

A swarm of hornets seemed to have chosen that moment to set-up-house in Jayce's stomach. This had never happened before. Ellie's bad-feelings usually came on suddenly. They worked out what was wrong, fixed it, and it was all over. And a headache had never been a symptom previously, either.

So, what happened at the lake? Jayce asked, trying to hide the worry in his voice.

That's just it. Nothing happened. I exchanged a few words with the old man; he fed the ducks, and I fed the ducks, and then he left, and I left. Absolutely nothing weird happened. My head was throbbing when I arrived home, closer to a migraine by then. So I went to bed and was out like a light in seconds.

Okay, but you've never mentioned the bad feeling causing pain in your head before. It's usually just in your stomach, isn't it?

Yep, Ellie replied, biting her lip. *And how the hell are we supposed to fix something we know nothing about?*

I wish I knew, beautiful girl Jayce said.

CHAPTER SEVEN

Bastian

Sebastian Evergreen, prince and heir to the Spring Court of the Fae Realm, pulled his pillow over his head in an attempt to block out the incessant knocking on the door to his rooms. How many times did he have to tell people that Saturdays were for sleeping in and shutting out the rest of the world? He had no intention of letting whoever was out there into his rooms. They could just go away and save whatever they felt was important and tell him on Monday.

Bastian breathed a sigh of relief when the persistent knocking stopped, only to be replaced by the voice of his best friend, Danis Farsight, yelling through the door. "For fate's sake, Bastian. Open the damned door. I know what you're thinking and there's no way I'm putting this off until Monday."

Bastian growled and rolled out of bed. Danis was the only person for whom he would break his do-not-disturb rule. With a frustrated sigh, he threw his hand out toward the door to remove the locking spell he'd placed on it the previous night. The second he heard the unlocking click, Danis burst into the room, his red hair sticking up in all directions. The frown on his friend's usually smiling face told Bastian that his news was *not* of the good variety.

"Okay, start talking. This better be good, Dan, or Fates help me—"

"It's about your fated mate," Danis burst out, and Bastian felt like he'd been punched in the gut.

"My what?" Bastian growled, figuring he might not have heard Danis right.

"Your. Fated. Mate." Danis repeated, enunciating each word slowly and clearly.

What the Fates did he care about some premonition about his supposed fated mate? He'd just turned sixteen for the love of pixies. No way he was ready to deal with any of this crap. Besides, most of Danis' visions were so far-fetched Bastian had grown accustomed to ignoring them.

"Okay, but this sounds like a conversation that requires coffee." Accepting that he'd have to listen to whatever Danis had to say, he headed over to the breakfast bar on the other side of his suite, where he knew the coffee maker would have already produced his favourite blend.

"Want one?" he threw over his shoulder at his friend, and Danis nodded gratefully.

"By the way, you look bloody awful. Was this another one of those premonitions? Must have been a doozy."

"You have no idea," Danis grumbled as he joined him, pouring himself a cup and adding milk and sugar.

"Well, it sounds like I'm about to. How about we get comfortable while you tell me everything? Just hang on a sec." Bastian turned back toward the door to his bedroom and reinstated the locking spell. Danis, on a Saturday, he might be able to do, but anyone else was not happening.

Walking back to his sitting area, Bastian flopped down onto the recliner and picked up his coffee. "Okay, shoot," he said, attempting to paste an interested look on his face.

Danis cleared his throat and threw Bastian an apologetic look before he opened his mouth. "Look, I get that you think we're too young to worry about stupid things like fated mates, but this is the exception. If we don't do something to help, she'll die before she's even born."

Bastian almost burst out laughing at the serious tone of his friend's voice. Maybe the premonitions coming in as often as they had been of late had pushed him over the edge. Because he was beginning to think that Danis was close to going off the deep end. Closer than Bastian had ever seen him. But then…

"Wait, you're serious, aren't you?" Bastian said, sobering and taking in Danis' grim face.

"As a heart attack. You need to listen, Bastian. Then tell me you don't care when you've heard it all."

Bastian sucked in a deep breath before giving his friend a nod. Fine, he'd listen first and then kick him out.

Danis began his tale in the Dragon Realm, and Bastian looked at his friend in shock. The Fae Realm had been cut off from the Dragon and Witch Realms for more than fifty years. How could anything or anyone in the Dragon realm affect a prince in the Fae Realm? But he kept listening, having promised Danis he would, and finding himself maybe a *bit* interested in how the story would play out.

Danis started with the story of Ellie, a half-mortal, half-witch, and her husband, a Dragon shifter named Jayce Raythawn. Bastian stiffened at the name Raythawn, recognising it as the name of the man responsible for the Fae Council's decision to shut themselves off. Danis went on to explain what Jayce and Ellie had done to save the Mortal Realm and bring peace between the Dragon and Witch Realms. Bastian had to admit that he admired the couple so far but still had no idea what any of it had to do with him.

When Danis told him that Ellie and Jayce had also defeated and killed Thomas Raythawn, the man responsible for so much grief across the realms, Bastian was completely caught up in the story. Yep—he was totally hooked.

"You saw all this in a premonition? That's crazy, man." Bastian said, taking a large gulp of his coffee and pointing to Danis' cup, suggesting he do the same. He figured his friend must be parched from all the story-telling.

"Hah! That's only the background stuff. It was just relayed in the form of pictures that flashed by, so I'd be up-to-date on everything," Danis said before taking another gulp and clearing his throat.

"Oh, and even though they have the same surname, Jayce was *not* Thomas' biological son. He carries none of the douchebag's DNA, which probably made it easier for him to actually kill the evil old bastard. Anyway, *now* is where it starts to get interesting. Turns out, Ellie is now pregnant with twin girls, and one of them is your fated mate."

"Wait, so you're telling me my fated mate is half dragon shifter, quarter witch and quarter mortal. By the Fates, Danis, the Fae Council would never accept her heritage as that of a suitable mate for a Prince of the Realm."

"Ah, but that's the thing. As long as we make sure your mate lives, who knows what laws will have changed by the time she turns eighteen? By then, you might be King of the Spring Court and can make new rules about who mates with whom." Danis chuckled, and Bastian had to admit his friend was right. Eighteen years was a long time.

"Okay, go on then. I'm dying to hear what you expect me to do about any of this."

"Yeah, well, this is where we veer off for a minute and learn who or what's causing all the problems. Otherwise known as the bad guy, who, of course, happens to be a Fae." Bastian groaned as his mind started to put some of the pieces together.

Danis went on to explain that Thomas was the cause of Valerius' parents' death, setting off a chain of events that led to Valerius being banished to the Mortal Realm. "Believing the twins to be of the same bloodline as Thomas, Valerius devised a plan to place a curse on Ellie. The curse works by convincing her brain she is no longer pregnant. Which means her body will slowly stop sending nourishment to the babies."

Danis paused and had another quick swig of his coffee. "That curse will be placed on Ellie sometime today, and Ellie and Jayce will have no idea of what's going on. They'll probably just assume the babies were stillborn due to some random pregnancy-related tragedy."

Bastian was struggling to contain the rage that was trying to break free. Even if one of these babies wasn't his fated mate, he was horrified by the mindless brutality it took to do something like this. They were babies for Fate's sake, and their parents were heroes who deserved better than to have to endure the pain of such senseless loss.

"So, I don't suppose this premonition also included suggestions for how we can stop the curse from being successful?" Bastian asked through gritted teeth.

Danis gave a huge sigh, obviously relieved Bastian might actually be considering getting involved. "Well, as a matter of fact, we've been tasked with helping Jayce to find the Oracle of the Fae. This Oracle apparently holds the cure for all curses, but demands a high price for sharing such information."

"Okay, so what's the price? Nothing we can't afford, surely?" Bastian said, brushing the matter aside as unimportant.

"Yeah, that's one of the things we won't know until we get there."

"Whadya mean *one* of the things? How many are there?"

"Well, there's the problem of *where* exactly we should look for the Oracle, not to mention how we can reach this Jayce Raythawn when there's no contact allowed between our realm and the Dragon realm. Oh, and we have to convince Jayce he needs our help *without* sharing the details of the prophecy."

Bastian lay his head against the back of the recliner and chewed on his lip. *Who in the Fae Realm might know anything about the information we needed? Maybe the old Priestess at the Temple of the Fates? She was older than dirt and probably knew way more than she'd ever tell. But with the right kind of persuasion... who knew?*

CHAPTER EIGHT

Ellie

*E*llie felt the tension in her body begin to melt away as she reclined in her comfy, king-size four-poster bed at the castle. Her head still ached, maybe even worse than before, but the thrumming in her bones had finally settled back into a dull ache. She took a deep breath and tried to focus solely on her babies. She couldn't remember feeling them move since Jayce had asked them to settle back at the aunts'. What if her stress levels had affected them somehow? She rubbed her belly with both hands, letting out a relieved sigh when she felt a foot move into place beneath each of her hands.

She smiled as Jayce appeared in the doorway carrying a tray with what looked like dinner for two. Thanking the Stars for the gazillionth time for bringing Jayce into her life, she smoothed the covers in front of her in anticipation of the tray's arrival. Jayce just grinned and shook his head.

"There is no way I'm putting this tray in front of you. How do you expect to pull it close enough that you won't be wearing half of it before you're finished?" They both looked at her giant belly and cracked up laughing.

Damn, it felt good to laugh. Ridiculous though it might sound, Ellie could remember laughing more in the months when they were on the run and fighting to survive than since they'd taken up residence in the Dragon Realm. Memories of sharing the danger, success and intrigue with Jayce back then made her realise how much she missed the closeness they'd experienced every day.

She smiled as she watched Jayce sit on the other side of the bed and place the tray between them. Then they sat in comfortable silence, munching on deliciously overstuffed sandwiches and Iridia's amazing honey cakes.

"So, I was thinking," Ellie finally said, rubbing her full belly with a contented smile. "We should probably start considering suitable names for these two wriggle-worts."

Jayce's face lit up. "Okay, so maybe I've been thinking about that already," he admitted with a grin. "What do you think about Angel for one of them? It's what we call them both most of the time, anyway.

What could be more fitting for a daughter of a Dragon Shifter and a Morwitch?"

Ellie clapped her hands in excitement. "Yesss... Angel is perfect!" she said, trying to think of an equally perfect name for Angel's sister. "Wait... what about Seraphim for Angel's sister? Maybe Sera for short. What do you think?"

"Angel and Sera, our two little angels" Jayce said, sounding just as excited as Ellie. "Perfect."

"So... Mr. Raythawn," Ellie said with a grin. "I can already picture you hovering over the girls like some giant, overprotective ogre. You'll probably breathe fire at any boy who looks their way."

Jayce's brow furrowed, his blue eyes flashing with mock indignation. "I'll have you know, Mrs Raythawn, that I am in complete control of my overprotective nature at all times," he replied, trying and failing to maintain a serious expression.

Ellie laughed, not letting him get away with his outrageous denial. "Riiight... so what was with the smoke coming out of your nostrils when one of the councillors accidentally bumped into me last week at the fundraiser?"

Jayce managed a sheepish smile. "That was... a momentary slip in my resolve," he said, pushing the tray aside and taking its place. "Besides, you know you love it."

"Says you..." Ellie whispered softly, her green eyes gentle as she gave him a coy look.

"Yes, you do. Whether you admit it or not! Although, I'm not averse to you *demonstrating* how much you love my assertiveness." Ellie squealed as Jayce rolled toward her, cradled her face in his hands, and placed his lips on hers. The kiss was electric, sending tingling sensations racing up and down her spine. Ellie basked in the glory of being kissed by this incredible man. She had to admit, she really did love everything about him. Not that she'd ever admit that to the arrogant arse.

When Jayce finally lifted his head, he caressed her swollen lips with his thumb. "Stars save us, I love you so much, Elle," he whispered, slightly breathless, his voice thick with emotion. "But you don't have to worry. I have plenty of love left over for our precious girls. And of course, any other future additions to our family."

Ellie almost choked at his last words. "Let me tell you something Mister. If you think I would ever even contemplate going through this—"

Jayce's kiss once again cut her off mid-sentence, and she knew without having to be told that he understood and accepted what she'd been about to say. For now, at least.

CHAPTER NINE

Bastian

Bastian's knee jiggled as he sat in the plush-looking but extremely uncomfortable chair in the Temple of the Fates Reception Room. He had no idea why he was nervous. He was a Crown Prince for fate's sake, but watching the ancient figure of the Priestess approach made him shiver with dread. Although he had to admit, he'd felt like that about almost everything since Danis delivered the details of his prophetic vision.

Bastian stood to bow to the old woman, not knowing the correct protocol for greeting a Priestess. The old Priestess smiled and waved him back to his chair, sitting across from him and sighing as she perched on the uncomfortable chair.

"Good day, Sebastian Evergreen, Crown Prince of

the Spring Court. I have lived in anticipation of this day for what feels like an eternity. What begins today will irrevocably change the future of the Magical Realms forever. Are you ready?"

Bastian just sat and stared at the old woman. How could she possibly know why he had come to see her? And wait—what he'd learned only yesterday she'd known for like… forever? He scratched his head and tried to think of a suitable response to the woman's words. "I—"

"That was a rhetorical question, young prince. I do not believe anyone would be ready for the journey you must undertake."

"But I don't understand. How do you know—"

"Danis Farsight's vision is part of a prophecy that has been a long time in the making. The journey you have been assigned will be long and arduous, but the rewards will far outweigh the sacrifices you must make. Did young Danis explain that you must not reveal the details of the prophecy to the dragon in order to convince him to help you?"

"Yes," Bastian replied, his scattered thoughts tumbling over each other in his confusion. So much for what he'd thought he was coming to tell or ask the Priestess. Apparently, she already knew way more than what Danis had told him.

He shook his head, trying to put some of his questions into words. This was bloody ridiculous. He kept expecting to wake up and find the whole thing had been a crazy dream. "Okay, so Danis also said we had to take the dragon with us to find the Oracle. But how do we find this Oracle? And how can I reach someone in the Dragon Realm when all contact between the realms has been forbidden for years?"

"Ah, yes. Of course, you would be unaware of the loopholes that were put in place when the law was passed. Did you honestly believe that the Fae rulers would allow life to go on in the Witch and Dragon Realms without the ability to monitor their political intents? That would be tantamount to blind trust, not something any ruler would ever embrace. But, like all rulers, they believed the law itself would prevent any Fae from attempting to cross realms. After all, the inhabitants of these other realms have been portrayed as vile creatures. Why would anyone want to risk visiting them?"

Bastian realised his jaw hung open and quickly snapped it shut. "So, you're saying I could just—"

"You can teleport to any Magical realm at any time. Yes, that's exactly what I'm saying." The Priestess looked up with a tilt of her head as if she was examining something unusual. "Actually, you show how well the law's assumptions have worked. Back when I was younger, young Fae creatures constantly moved between worlds while creating chaos wherever they went."

Okay, so he could just teleport to the Dragon Realm and find this Jayce Raythawn. He'd think about the logistics of that later. So, what else did he need to find out from the Priestess again? Oh yeah, where to find this damned Oracle. Before he could even open his mouth to ask, the Priestess sighed.

"Yes, I can see that you grow impatient to leave. But first, there are two things I must share with you. As you are undoubtedly aware, it is extremely dangerous to portal into a place you've never visited or at least seen. It has been eons since I visited the Dragon Realm, but I can place an image of the Dragon Council grounds as they were then into your mind. Places like that rarely change."

Bastian staggered slightly as the image appeared in his brain. "Bloody hell, woman, how did—?"

The old Priestess chuckled again and raised her hand. "You do not need to know the how; in this situation, the why is sufficient justification for the deed."

"Fine. So, what's the second thing then?" Bastian huffed, rubbing his temple. He hated only being told half of a story, which he was pretty sure was happening here.

"To find the Oracle of the Fae, you must travel to Brevis, a realm that exists solely to service those who have a great need."

"Wait…what? How the hell…?" Bastian felt ready to burst. Sure, he'd heard of this Brevis realm. Apparently, it used to serve as a neutral meeting place for the rulers of the magical realms to discuss situations that might affect other races. But the entrance had been sealed years ago. Hadn't it? Or was this just another one of those loopholes the Priestess had mentioned earlier?

"Ahhh... I see you are beginning to develop a better picture of what's really going on. As you have probably guessed, the entrance is only sealed by a spell. It continues to exist and will function perfectly once the spell is reversed."

Bastian stood up and started pacing, needing to release some of the pent-up frustration brought on by the Priestess' revelations. "So everything I thought I knew about the Fae Realm's separation from the other Magical Realms is a load of crap? Why the massive ruse?"

The old Priestess simply raised her hands and dropped them in her lap, as if answering that question presented a quandary she couldn't begin to fathom. "I have always believed that one of the more sensible and forward-thinking rulers understood the implications of making the law permanent and irreversible, insisting that the doors remain closed but not destroyed. Thank the fates someone did."

Bastian stopped pacing and turned to look into the eyes of the Priestess for the first time, sucking in a breath at the sight of the constantly changing colours of her irises. Bastian was beginning to suspect that this old woman was far more powerful than anyone he'd ever met. He found himself wishing he had the time to sit and discuss some of the secrets he was sure the old woman held.

"Right, so just to be clear. First, I need to teleport into the Dragon Realm and find this Jayce Raythawn. Then, I need to convince him to believe what a complete stranger is telling him and then agree to meet said stranger on Brevis. Oh, and all while not telling him what's going on or why he needs to do it."

The Priestess nodded, biting her lip as if trying to hide her smile.

"Then, I need to come back to the fae Realm, meet up with Danis, and try to work out how to break the spell currently sealing the entrance to Brevis. Does that all sound about right? No other pearls of wisdom to assist us in achieving this miracle?"

The Priestess actually smiled and nodded her head in Bastian's direction. "Good luck, young prince. May the Fates guide you and keep you safe."

Then, before Bastian could say another word, the Priestess stood and headed back to wherever she'd come from.

CHAPTER TEN

Jayce

Jayce paced the floor of his office in the Dragon Council chamber. He knew in his gut that something more than the usual *bad-feeling* thing was going on with Ellie. Not that she'd ever tell him. She was always more concerned with how things affected others than her own well-being. Although she'd admitted that the bad-feeling had only dulled instead of going away, it was the headaches that worried him the most.

He growled in frustration. Why couldn't Ellie see that anything that affected *her* now affected the well-being of their babies as well? Damnit, he would have to make her understand that she needed to tell him about even the slightest things that might affect her as well as the babies.

He'd just sat down at his desk to finish the work he'd come in to do when the door flew open, and his best-friend, Rhett, stood in the doorway. "Did you forget how to knock?" Jayce growled.

"Okay, sorry for the interruption, but you need to come with me *right now*," Rhett was panting as if he'd just run a marathon.

"What the—?"

Rhett held his hand up and shook his head. "Nope. Trust me, you need to see this to believe it. Now get up and follow me."

"Fine," Jayce huffed, pushing back his chair and following the fast-retreating Rhett out the door. "But this better be good, mate, or—"

"Jayce, for Star's sake, will you just shut up and move your arse. This is important."

"Yeah, yeah, whatever. I feel like I'm in a spy novel or something equally ridiculous."

Rhett chuckled and turned back to look at him. "You have no idea…"

They reached the door leading to the courtyard, but instead of going out, Rhett opened the door to the left and ushered him into a rarely used, extremely dusty storeroom. On the far side of the room, he could just make out the silhouette of a man in a dark cloak. The man stood very still and appeared to be looking out of the small, grimy window in front of him.

Rhett cleared his throat, and the man turned

quickly. "Ummm… excuse me, Sebastian? This is Jayce Raythawn."

The man smiled, throwing back the hood of his cloak with a sigh. "Thank the fates I found you. Please excuse the dramatics, but I felt it best not to announce my arrival. I was fortunate enough to stumble across your friend, Rhett, who agreed to help me. My name is Sebastian Evergreen, and I am the Crown Prince of the Spring Court in the Fae Realm."

Jayce knew he was staring, but he couldn't stop. The man, or rather the boy, who stood before him could only be described as beautiful. His silver-white hair fell to his shoulders, perfectly matching his sparkling silver eyes. But the most astonishing thing was his ears. They were pointed at the top instead of round.

Holy, snapping Stars above, the boy was an elf. Not that Jayce had ever seen one before, but he'd read enough history books to know he was looking at a member of the long-hidden race.

"Right…" was all Jayce felt capable of saying. So many questions were tumbling inside his head that he didn't know where to start.

Bastian chuckled and held out his hand. "Well met, Jayce Raythawn Dragon Shifter," Jayce shook the boy's hand and studied his beautiful face in fascination. "I am here to aid you with an urgent matter I'm not sure you are even aware of. Unfortunately, I am bound not to reveal the who and the why, but I must help you with the how and the where."

Jayce finally felt his brain start to re-engage, and he shook his head. "I'm sorry, maybe it's just my befuddled brain, but what you just said made absolutely no sense. But I do think the *urgent matter* part requires a bit more explanation, *especially* where it involves a Dragon shifter and a Fae prince working together."

Rhett cleared his throat again, and Jayce looked around in surprise. He'd forgotten his friend was still there. "I'm thinking this conversation might go better if we all sit around the table and discuss things in a slightly more comfortable environment." Jayce smiled as he saw that Rhett had cleaned off a table and put three chairs around it. "But first… what'll it be? Coffee, tea, or water?"

Jayce waved Sebastian towards a chair and pulled one out for himself. "Yeah, coffee sounds good. Thanks, Rhett."

"A water would be great, thank you," Sebastian said as he took off the heavy cape and folded it over the back of his chair. At least the guy wore simple jeans and a t-shirt, not the elven finery Jayce had seen in history books—a tiny bit of normalcy amid what felt like a catastrophe about to unfold.

They sat and stared at each other for a moment as if neither were sure where to start.

Finally, Bastian ran his hand through his silver-white hair and sighed. "No matter how many times I rehearsed what to say when we finally met, I still don't know how I'm going to convince you to come with me without being able to tell you why. Would it help if I told you the entire situation involves a prophecy?"

Jayce felt the blood freeze in his veins. *Bloody prophecies!* He'd hoped and prayed to be done with them for this lifetime. Apparently not. "Yep. *Now* everything makes perfect sense."

Bastian

BASTIAN WATCHED the expressions flit across the dragon shifter's face in fascination. A plethora of emotions seemed to battle for supremacy before Jayce's face settled into resigned acceptance. Apparently, whatever his previous experiences with prophecies had involved, the memories were far from pleasant.

"Okay, so first off, please call me Bastian. Sebastian is associated with way too much pomp and ceremony."

Jayce chuckled and nodded in understanding. "No worries. So, can you tell me how and why you're involved in whatever this is?"

Bastian shook his head, feeling almost as frustrated as Jayce looked. "Unfortunately, that part is attached way too closely to the actual prophecy. But I can tell you that it involves the safety and well-being of your family."

Jayce blanched and looked ready to throw up. "Then the rest doesn't matter. Just tell me where and when, and we can get started. Nothing is more important than my family, and I will have to trust that you have our best interests at heart."

Bastian immediately warmed to Jayce at his words. His selflessness when it came to his family was truly admirable. That he would blindly follow a total stranger's lead to ensure the safety of his family was a rare trait indeed. "Okay, so I believe you are familiar with the realm known as Brevis?"

Jayce groaned, put his elbows on the table, and dropped his head into his hands. Just then, the door opened, and Rhett stepped in, carrying a coffee and two bottles of water.

"Please tell me I didn't just hear the word Brevis?" Rhett said, sitting down at the table and handing out the drinks. "Although, from the look of Jayce, I'm going to assume I heard right."

Bastian frowned, unsure what to say next. He'd heard a few stories about Jayce needing to travel to Brevis before, but there had never been many details. He was guessing the memories weren't pleasant ones.

"Can you at least tell me what we need from Brevis? The one thing I do know for sure is that there always has to be a need." Jayce muttered, his words slightly garbled with his head still in his hands.

"We need to find the Oracle of the Fae."

Jayce lifted his head, and the look in his eyes made Bastian's skin crawl. *What the fates had happened to this man on Brevis?*

"Of course we do. For the Star's sake, why does everything related to fixing problems always have to be hidden somewhere on Brevis?"

"So, it's that bad then?" Bastian asked, not sure he really wanted to know.

Jayce blew out a long, slow breath and ran his hands through his hair. "Well, I guess it's not so much Brevis that's the problem. Let's just say that my previous visits have ended up being a tad traumatic."

"Well, I was told by an old Priestess that the Oracle can definitely be found on Brevis," Bastian said and shrugged. "So that's where we need to go."

"Wait," Jayce said, eyes boring directly into Bastian's. "I know I said I'd do anything to protect my family, but I'm really struggling to understand why a Fae prince and a Fae Oracle are involved with ensuring the safety of a dragon's family."

"Okay, so let me ask you something. From your earlier reaction when I mentioned a prophecy, I assume you've had to deal with at least one before today? Were you never told the where and when you had to search for answers while the who and why were withheld?"

"Yeah, yeah," Jayce said, his eyes dropping to his coffee while his face held a cheeky grin. "But you can't blame a man for trying to dig for any extra information available."

Bastian chuckled and breathed a sigh of relief, knowing he'd done the right thing coming to find Jayce. "Okay, so I've learned that the entrance to Brevis in the Fae realm has been concealed behind a spell for the last fifty years. I plan to return home, break the spell, and then myself and my friend Danis will be headed to Brevis."

"Hang on a minute," Rhett said, pulling their attention to the man seated at the other end of the table. "If Bastian is taking a friend, then I'm going too. Someone needs to have your back—"

Jayce immediately shook his head. "No, Rhett, I'm sorry, but I need you to stay here and keep an eye on Ellie. You know she's not been well, and I don't want her worrying about any of this. I'll tell her I have to attend a meeting with the head of the Witch Council on Brevis, which she knows has always been considered neutral ground for meetings in the past."

Bastian had to work to conceal his shock at Jayce's words about Ellie being sick already. According to Danis, the curse had been placed on Ellie only twenty-four hours ago. Who knew how quickly her brain would convince her body to stop nourishing the babies? And they had no idea how long it would take to find the Oracle and get the cure.

Bastian stood and pulled his cloak from the back of the chair. "I'm sorry, but we need to get moving as soon as possible. I understand that you don't know me nor have any reason to trust me, but the stakes are too high to delay our departure any longer. I've heard that the entrances to Brevis are keyed to each particular race, so I will need to return to the Fae Realm in order to travel. Is this true?" At Jayce's nod of acknowledgement he went on. " Then I was hoping we could arrange to meet on Brevis in, let's say, four hours?"

Looking from Jayce to Rhett as he wrapped the long cloak around himself and secured it at the neck, Bastion reached into a hidden pocket, pulling out the amulet he had brought with him for Jayce. "You'll need to be holding this seeking amulet once you land on Brevis, in case we need to find each other. It will activate when held in your hand and call to the one I'll be carrying."

Jayce took the amulet from Bastian and slipped it into his pocket. Bastian nodded, knowing he'd done all he could. Now, it was up to Jayce to decide whether he'd pick up the ball and run with it. Somehow, even though he'd only known Jayce for such a short time, Bastian knew the father-to-be would do whatever he deemed necessary to keep his family safe.

He was about to teleport home when Jayce's face broke into a crafty grin. "Wait... before you go, I'll just give you the heads-up I wish someone had given me before the first time I travelled to Brevis via the

Aqueous Flow. When the voice says breathe, don't argue, just do it. Guess it's your turn to trust the words of a perfect stranger."

Bastian cocked his head and nodded at Jayce before teleporting out of the Dragon Realm toward home.

CHAPTER ELEVEN

Ellie

*E*llie rubbed her belly and sipped on the raspberry tea Iridia had made her. She was almost finished, and her head did seem to be aching a little less. She didn't understand what was going on. It almost felt like the left and right sides of her brain were at war with each other, and neither was prepared to back down.

"Feeling better, dear? Iridia asked. "If not, maybe you could ask Jayce to help you cast a healing spell. You've done that together before, haven't you?"

Ellie smiled at the memory of the first time they'd done it. Jayce had been desperately trying to keep her awake long enough to repeat the words of the spell after him. They'd had no idea at the time that casting the spell together had increased its potency exponentially. She'd not only been completely healed by the magic, but the scar had looked at least six months old after only a few hours.

"Yes, we have—a few times, actually. But I don't want to risk the spell affecting the babies. It's only a headache; I'm sure it will ease eventually. And the tea has helped, thank you." Ellie smiled at Jayce's mother, wanting to erase the worried frown the older woman wore. She hated people worrying about her and decided right there and then not to show any more signs of the ongoing pain to anyone.

Iridia smiled and noticed her almost empty cup. "Well then, would you like another one? Might just do the trick, eh?"

Ellie quickly emptied the cup and handed it to the older woman. "Thanks, Iridia, that would be lovely," Ellie replied, pleased that the smile on Iridia's face had replaced the earlier frown. *Yay, one less thing to worry about.*

"Ooh, do you think I could have one of those too, please, Iridia?" Mum's voice preceded her arrival as she appeared in the doorway—*and yes, appear was exactly what she did.* Ellie shook her head at her mother's usual flamboyant entrance. The older witch loved to arrive out of the blue with a flourish and leave the same way. *Overly theatrical much?*

"It's raspberry tea?" Iridia called over her shoulder as she headed for the kitchen.

"Perfect, thanks, Dia," her mum said as she dropped

into the lounge chair next to Ellie. "And how are you, my sweet? Fully recovered from yesterday's traumatic events?"

"Yep," Ellie said, pasting a smile onto her face to conceal the lie. "Everything is fine. The raspberry tea seems to have finally fixed the headache."

Her mother breathed out a heavy sigh. "Well, thank the Stars for that. I was worried something else was wrong, what with the headache not being a usual symptom of the bad feeling."

"Yeah, well…" Ellie sat up straighter in her chair as a memory from before all this latest crap happened came back to her. "By the way, I've been meaning to ask you something. The other day, before we went to the mortal realm, something weird happened with my magic."

Mum stiffened in her chair. "Something weird like what?"

"Well, it started with this tingling sensation. It felt like I was being flooded with energy, and then my hands started to glow and pulsate."

"Go on," her mum prompted, her brows drawn into a frown.

"And then the light kind of exploded out of me. I guess it was a bit like when I use a power thrust. But I had no control over any of it."

"Okay… and this all happened before the whole bad feeling and headache thing? Why didn't you say anything earlier?"

"Honestly, I'd forgotten all about it until now. I remember thinking I'd ask you if it was a normal part of carrying magical babies. But, well…you know what pregnancy brain is like. Thoughts just evaporate all the time."

Ellie suddenly felt sick as she watched her mother stand up and begin to pace. She knew her mother only did this when she was really worried. *So, it looked like the whole exploding magic thing wasn't the norm? How unusual... not!*

As if realising what she'd done, her mum stopped pacing and turned to Ellie with apologetic eyes. "Oh, I'm so sorry, honey. I didn't mean to scare you. It's just… well, I've never heard of this happening during a pregnancy. But wait, before you start to panic, I've also never known a witch carrying twins, let alone half-dragon shifter twins."

"Okay, what did I miss?" Iridia asked as she re-entered the room carrying a tray with three cups of tea and some cakes. "You two look about ready to hurl chunks."

Ellie couldn't hold back the laugh that erupted at Iridia's blunt but descriptive words. She had a sneaking suspicion that the older woman had used those words deliberately to relieve some of the tension in the air. *Mission accomplished, Iridia!*

Mum took her tea from the tray and sat down, looking slightly less stressed, as she answered Iridia's question. "Ellie's magic has been acting weird. Nothing

I've ever heard of before." She turned back to face Ellie. "But I suppose under the circumstances, we'll just have to hope it was an anomaly that won't happen again. But if anything like it *does* happen again, you need to tell me immediately. Okay?"

Ellie nodded and gratefully accepted the tea and a small cake from Iridia. Damnit, she was so sick of the *no-one-ever-heard-of-that* response to the things that constantly happened to her and Jayce. There needed to be some kind of instruction manual that explained why shit happened! But then, maybe all the answers had been in the Book of Time they'd found on Brevis and then forgone the opportunity to open. Somehow, getting those answers had not been worth the cost of being trapped in an underground cavern on Brevis for all eternity.

All thoughts of what they'd been discussing flew out of Ellie's head as she heard Jayce's dragon claws thud against the cobblestones out front. Her man was home, and nothing else mattered.

Jayce

MORPHING back into his human form, Jayce reviewed everything he needed to do in his head for the last time. Ellie was used to him shutting down their link while he was at work, but now that he was home, one wrong thought would blow everything. He only had three hours to spend with Ellie before he needed to leave for Brevis, having wasted a precious hour finishing up his Council work. He'd decided to tell her that a last-minute emergency meeting with the Witch Council had been called, and he had to attend. The fact that Brevis was where these meetings had historically been held was just a bonus.

He looked up to see Ellie walking toward him, a broad smile on her beautiful face. He hated that he would be responsible for turning that smile into disappointment.

"What's this? I haven't been gone that long, have I? Although I'm definitely not complaining about my wife greeting me on my arrival home." Jayce laughed and opened his arms as Ellie practically threw herself at him. "Wait... is everything okay? Are you and the babies—"

Ellie's lips on his stopped the flow of words instantly. As always, Ellie's kiss transported him somewhere quiet and safe, where he floated in blissful contentment. Until the reality of their current predicament burst through his peaceful existence, and he groaned in disappointment.

"Jayce, what's wrong? And don't even try to give me

the old *oh-it's-nothing* routine when I distinctly heard a groan during our kiss. So, spit it out!"

Jayce couldn't hold back the chuckle that sneaked out at Ellie's bossy demands. She was always a spitfire, but lately, her pregnancy hormones seemed to have all her emotions on a continuous rollercoaster. Ellie's dark scowl at his chuckle was enough to tell him he was teetering on thin ice.

"Sorry, baby," he said, holding her at arm's length. "I groaned because I knew I had to disappoint you. I know I said I only had to work those couple of hours, and then we'd have a few days off together, but a call came in from Helena, the head of the Witch Council, while I was at work. Apparently, there's some emergency that can only be discussed on Brevis. The meeting is tonight, and there's no way I can get out of it."

Jayce watched the gamut of emotions that played over Ellie's expressive face, holding his breath as he waited for her final reaction. Disappointment, worry, acceptance and then resignation. He breathed a sigh of relief that she hadn't insisted on going with him. He knew it was something she would have done before the pregnancy, but apparently, she'd finally accepted her limitations, along with their temporary nature.

"Fine," she huffed. "But if I wasn't pregnant—"

This time, it was Jayce who silenced her words. Still kissing her, he reached down under her knees and lifted her into his arms.

Maybe we should save the arguing for a time when we have more than a few hours together. Right now, I have way more important things to... discuss with my beautiful wife.

Jayce's heart sang at Ellie's school-girl giggle. Striding past Iridia and Yvette, where the two sat chuckling on the lounge, he headed for their room, their sanctuary from the outside world. He intended to show the amazing woman in his arms just how much he loved her before he had to leave for Brevis.

CHAPTER TWELVE

Bastian

Bastian went in search of Danis as soon as he returned to the Fae Realm. His friend knew better than anyone that time was of the essence and had promised to find what he could about the spell protecting the entrance to Brevis while Bastian was gone. Bastian could only hope Danis had found someone who might be able to help them.

Determined to ignore the stares and whispers, Bastian strode purposefully through the castle. So maybe he didn't usually leave his rooms on the weekend—*okay, fine... so he never did*—but surely these people had something more important to gossip about than the crown prince being out and about on a Saturday. Bastion did, however, manage a grin at the fact that no one had been stupid enough to either approach him or attempt to speak to him. At least some things remained sacred.

"Bastian, wait up," a voice called from behind him. He turned, ready to abuse the person stupid enough to cross the sacred line he'd just been thinking about. But at the sight of Danis racing toward him, he let the anger go. Everyone knew that the same rules didn't apply to Danis. *Well, most of the time, anyway.*

"How did the visit go?" Danis asked, slightly out of breath from hurrying to catch up to Bastian. "Any hitches in the plan I should know about?"

"Nope. We are all good to go. In fact, we're meeting Jayce on Brevis in just under four hours. So I hope you got some answers about how to get past the spell at the entrance?"

Danis scratched his head and smiled sheepishly. "Yeah, about that. Apparently, your father is the only person with the answers we need. So, how do you feel about telling the King what's going on?"

"Are you serious?" Bastian almost choked on his words. "My father will hear the word Dragon and refuse to listen to another word. Unless the prophecy threatened the Fae Realm or its inhabitants, he'd just wave us away and tell us to forget it. I wasn't even planning on telling him we were leaving the realm, seeing we're already guaranteed not to be disturbed for the entire weekend. There must be someone else who can help us?"

Danis opened his mouth as if to say something, then

shook his head and closed it again. He actually managed to look guilty, for fate's sake.

"What?" Bastian prompted, putting his hand on his friend's shoulder. "What did you think of that you don't want to tell me?"

Danis looked at the floor and shrugged. "I was thinking that my mum might be able to unravel the spell or something. You know how good she is with anything spell-related. But I don't want her to get into trouble if this all blows up."

Bastian nodded and tried to suppress the excitement at Danis' idea. Bastian knew Danis' mum, Bella, well enough to believe she would try to help them. She was kind-hearted and generous to a fault. In fact, Bastian had often wished he could trade places with Danis and assume his friend's far less complicated existence. Being the heir to the Spring Court was not a future Bastian would have chosen for himself.

"Okay," Bastian finally answered with a huge sigh. "I get what you're saying, and I totally agree. But I think maybe we should tell her the whole story and let her decide what to do, with no pressure either way. Your mum is definitely someone I'd like to have on our side. Besides, I guess it would be good if someone knew where we were going. You know, in case something goes wrong."

Danis sighed and nodded again. "Okay. I can't say I'm not relieved that Mum will know where we went.

I'd hate to just disappear and have her never know what happened to us."

They walked in silence, each lost in their own thoughts, as they headed for the Farsight suite of rooms in the castle's east wing. As the greatest seer of their time, Bella Farsight, Danis' mother, was the Fae King's right hand. Her incredible ability with spellcraft was a less publicised skill, but she was brilliant, nonetheless. Bastian sent a silent prayer to the fates that she would be able to help them.

The minute they stepped inside the Farsight suite of rooms, Bastian felt some of the constant tension he carried lessen. It had always been this way; the space was somehow imbued with the calm ambience surrounding Bella Farsight.

"Hey, Mum, are you here?" Danis called as they entered the lavishly designed rooms. Although lavish, the rooms were decorated with soft, pastel colours that portrayed comfort rather than opulence.

"Danis, my darling," a voice crooned from the next room. "What are you doing—wait, is that Prince Sebastian? Out of his rooms on a Saturday? Fates, this must be important." She smirked and winked at Bastian, and his embarrassment at her words quickly ebbed. He hated that people thought him a pompous arsehole because he spent all weekend locked away in his rooms. But Bella knew it was Bastian's way of coping with the otherwise constant demands of his position.

"Right, I get the feeling I'm going to need to be

sitting down with a cup of tea for this conversation. I don't think I can recall ever seeing you two looking so... serious? Especially at the same time. How about you boys settle in my office while I arrange refreshments. What would you like, juice or lemonade?"

"Either would be great," Bastian said, and Danis absently nodded his agreement. Bastian didn't miss the worry in Bella's eyes before he and Danis turned and headed for her office.

By the time they reached Bella's office and sat down on the comfy lounge, Bastian felt like his head was ready to explode. He desperately needed answers to some of the never-ending questions tumbling around in his brain, hating that they were forced to sit around waiting while fates knew what was happening to those poor babies.

Yeah, yeah, he knew that thinking about an unborn baby as his fated mate was about as weird as weird could get, so he decided then and there not to refer to the two as the same person. He would do whatever was necessary to break the curse for Ellie, Jayce and their babies' sake. No way he could ever consider an unborn baby as his fated mate. But the reality of how this situation could affect his future was becoming more apparent with every passing moment.

That reality plagued his thoughts until all others were silenced. Sure, he knew people who had never found their fated mates and had instead settled for a chosen mate. But *settled for* were the words that made his blood run cold. His own parents were a perfect example of what a relationship that lacked the bond of a fated mate looked like. They were both always polite to each other, smiling and appearing to all the worlds as if they were happy, but Bastian knew better.

After fulfilling her duty as Queen and providing the Spring Court with an heir, Bastian's mother, Sasha Evergreen, had devoted her life to performing all her required Queenly duties except those of a loving mother and wife. Because of his mother's neglect, Bastian's father sought love and companionship from sources outside their marriage. Not that Bastian blamed the old King. How could he, when he had sought a similar kind of emotional support from the loving family of his best friend Danis?

Now *there* was a great example of the love resulting from the bond between fated mates. Bella and William Farsight had been inseparable since they first met as teenagers. When they married, William had even agreed to take on Bella's surname so her family line would continue. Danis was their youngest child, while his three much older siblings were off living their own lives and following their own dreams.

So... the bottom line of all these thoughts? Bastian would do anything within his power to ensure those babies survived and grew up to become whoever fate intended them to be. Bastian would deal with the issue of whether he had a fated mate sometime in the far distant future.

Bella bustled into the room with a tray holding refreshments, placing it on her desk and turning to them with a smile. "Help yourselves, boys. Now I'm dying to know what has you two in this state of agitated suspense. What the fates is going on?"

Danis reached for a glass of juice, gulped it down, then sucked in a deep breath before launching into the details of his vision followed by everything that had happened since. Bella's eyes had grown wide with horror, then sadness and finally resolve before Danis had finished speaking.

Bastian was sure his heart would burst if Bella didn't speak soon. "So... can you help us?" he asked softly. "I mean, we don't want to be the cause of you getting into trouble, so it's okay if you can't. But—"

Bella held up her hand and gave Bastian a sad smile. "Have I told you two how proud I am of the amazing young men you've become? The fact that you would even consider going to these lengths to help not only strangers, but also those of a race long shunned and disconnected from our own, is evidence of your incredible strength of character and selfless resolve. I would be honoured to help in any way I can. Which just so happens to be way more than you'd imagine."

Danis jumped up from his seat and ran behind the desk to hug his mother. "You are the best. But seriously? Do you know something that can help us? Anything would be great about now."

Bastian watched the smile on Bella's face morph

into a wicked grin. Whatever secret she was about to share filled her with excited energy. "Well, would it help to know that *I* was the one who spelled the entrance to Brevis? Which means I know both its location *and* the reversing spell."

Bastian sat in stunned silence as his eyes met Bella's. She seemed to know every thought he'd had since learning about the threat to his future happiness, her excitement because she knew what helping them could mean. "Thank you so much, Bella," he said, his voice gruff with emotion. "This means everything—"

"I know exactly what this means to you, son. As only someone who has spent her life with her own fated mate can," Bella's eyes glistened with tears to match his own. "Now… time to get organised. Do you have supplies for the trip? I think you should pack for at least three days just to be safe."

"Three days?" Danis looked at Bastian in horror. "What the blazes is going to take that long?"

Bella smiled and patted her son's hand. "Did you really think you'd just land on Brevis, find the Oracle and perform whatever tasks he sets in a day? Seriously, Danis, this is like a quest of old. And they were always bigger and more difficult than they appeared at the start. I'll do my best to cover your absence from court. Any suggestions for where I might say you are?"

This was one of the questions that had been tumbling around in Bastian's brain, and he'd already come up with an idea. "How about saying you sent us to the Summer Court for some instruction on intricate spellcraft with Harris?" Harris was Danis' eldest brother, and Bastian knew the man would do anything for his baby brother and his mother. As a renowned master of spellcraft in his own right, it would make sense for the boys to spend time learning from him.

"Brilliant!" Bella grinned and rubbed her hands together like a villain with a masterplan. Something about her thrilled anticipation was contagious and Bastian began to consider the reality of what Bella had aptly called their quest, surprised to find he was looking forward to the adventure.

He smiled at the glow of his own excitement reflected in Danis' eyes, and his heart began to pound from the adrenaline coursing through his body. This was really going to happen. They were going to Brevis to find the Oracle and break a curse!

CHAPTER THIRTEEN

Jayce

Jayce stood on the edge of the pool that led to the Aqueous Flow and stared into its azure blue, crystal clear depths. He tried to suppress the memories of his previous experiences within the flow, but they barrelled into him regardless. Recalling the previously murky brown depths of the pool, compliments of the taint Thomas had planted within it, made him shiver. That had been the first time.

Although the second time he'd travelled the pool had appeared similar to the way it looked now, the memory of the emotionless automaton teetering on the brink of insanity he'd been at the time had nausea rising in his throat.

Stop it, you moron. That's all in the past. How about you just get on with fixing whatever problem looms in the future?

Wow… it had been a long time since that nagging little voice had reared its ugly head. He'd always hated it, so hadn't missed it since it had stopped— however long ago that was. A sense of foreboding filled him at the little voice's untimely return. Its presence was associated with the fear and apprehension he and Ellie had endured while battling the darkness of Thomas Raythawn.

Before the stupid voice could chastise him again for wasting time, he sucked in a deep breath and dived into the pool.

Bastian

BASTIAN HAD WATCHED in awe as Bella worked her magic on the entrance to Brevis as if it were nothing. They had agreed that Bella should remove the spell, usher the two boys into the previously hidden room, and then immediately restore the lock behind them. Bastian was still reeling from the knowledge that the spelled entrance had sat less than fifty metres from his rooms his entire life. Not that there had ever been any sign of a hidden room behind what appeared to be an unbroken wall.

Bastian summoned a light orb in his hand and looked around the small room in awe. Not that there was much to see. The small round pool Bella had explained they would use to travel to Brevis sat proudly in the centre of the room. Unfortunately, Bella had no experience using the Aqueous Flow. Not being a member of the ruling Fae Council at the time, she'd never heard of it before she'd been asked to seal the entrance.

But it was the intricately decorated walls surrounding the pool that held Bastian's fascinated attention. They depicted scenes from the past, where witches, dragons and Fae greeted each other with smiles and back slaps. He'd never seen such a beautiful rendition of a dragon, let alone one whose scales shone as gold as the sun. The walls were covered in images of members of the three races laughing, drinking and sometimes in heated discussions around tables.

"Whoa... this is pretty amazing. Who knew this relic from the past was sitting here the whole time? I must have walked past this spot a gazillion times," Danis whispered as they both stood transfixed before the wall's revelations.

Bastian chuckled and put his hand on his friend's shoulder. "Why are you whispering? I don't think we need to worry about being heard. Somehow, I think the spell would obliterate any sound along with the sight of the room."

Danis seemed to snap out of his transfixed state at Bastian's words and turned to stare into the crystal-clear waters of the pool. He scratched his head and turned to Bastian with a frown.

"Ummm… what was it Jayce said about breathing in there?" He reached into the pool and ran his hands through the water. "Because last time I checked, water was for swimming and air was for breathing…"

Bastian just shrugged and studied the water as Danis had done. "Jayce's exact words were *'when the voice says to breathe, don't argue, just do it'*. Apart from that, I know as much as you do about what voice, what and when to breathe and what the fates to expect."

Bastian cinched his backpack a little tighter and stepped up onto the rim of the pool. "But standing around thinking about it won't change anything. Jayce also said it was time for us to invest in some of the blind trust we were asking him to embrace." Bastian reached down and pulled his friend up beside him. So… I guess I'll see you on the other side… or not. Good luck, my friend."

Without another word, Bastian dived into the pool, sending a prayer to the Fates that it wouldn't be the last time he saw his lifelong best friend.

Danis

WITH HIS EYES fixed on the spot where Bastian had entered the pool and quickly disappeared from sight, Danis sucked in a huge breath and considered his options. He'd never considered himself a coward, but then he'd also never been an adrenaline junky who took blind risks without good reason.

Okay... so maybe it was time to question why he was doing this. The fact that he'd had the vision didn't necessarily mean he had to go on the quest. The prophecy had been specific about the need for Jayce and Bastian to go, as they would both be impacted by the predicted outcome. But Danis would be risking everything for no other reason than his friendship with Bastian.

He stood on the rim of the pool, replaying some of the more memorable moments of his friendship with Sebastian Evergreen. If he were honest, he'd have to admit that Bastian had become more of a brother than his blood siblings had ever been. The two boys had been inseparable since they first met as toddlers, and Danis couldn't imagine his life without Bastian in it.

And there it was! He breathed a huge sigh of relief

at his inner revelation. No matter what the outcome of this quest, Danis did not want to live in a world without his best friend. In fact, now that he was thinking straight again, he couldn't believe he'd even considered not going with Bastian to Brevis. Pushing away the shame threatening to wash over him, he cinched his backpack as Bastian had and sucked in a deep breath.

See you soon, my brother-by-another-mother, Danis thought as he dived into whatever future the Fates deemed necessary for his sorry arse.

CHAPTER FOURTEEN

Jayce

$\mathcal{U}$nsure how long he'd been floating in the silent void, Jayce was relieved when the familiar voice of the Aqueous entered his head.

Breathe, the voice said, and Jayce fought against the instinctual urge to argue.

He knew how the flow worked. The water would turn to air as soon as he breathed in. Still, the logical part of his brain insisted he would drown. Pushing the thought aside, he opened his mouth and sucked the air into his lungs.

Ah... welcome back, Son of the Stars and Leader of the Dragon Council. It has been long since your last need to travel. What do you require from Brevis this time?

I need to find the Oracle of the Fae.

The voice fell silent for a moment. *But you are not*

Fae. Why does a dragon seek the Oracle, and why do you believe you will find them on Brevis?

Because a prophecy involving my family foretold of the need to find the Oracle of the Fae. So... you know the drill. I have a need that Brevis must fulfil.

The voice chuckled. *Indeed, I must. Good luck on your Quest, Jayce Raythawn.*

Wait... what Quest? Nobody said anything about a quest...?

Silence once again filled the void surrounding him. Great, no answers as usual. Fine, he'd just have to be patient. But this Prince Sebastian had better have some answers if he expected Jayce to blindly follow him on what had apparently been labelled some kind of Fate's forsaken quest!

Bastian

TOTALLY OBLIVIOUS TO what he should expect to happen next, Bastian cursed himself for not asking Jayce for more details about travelling in this Aqueous Flow. His chest had started to burn from holding his breath, and he was beginning to question whether the dragon had invented the advice he'd given Bastian and was now laughing over the gullible Fae Prince's demise. Even worse, he'd led his best friend into this death trap like a lamb to the slaughter.

Breathe, a husky voice crooned in his head.

Wait, was that the voice Jayce had said to obey? Or was it just some hallucination his brain had invented to hurry along the drowning process?

Yeah... about that... Bastian's mind replied to the voice.

If you do not breathe, you will die, the voice answered in its monotonous tone.

So, we're not going to discuss the fact that if I do breathe, I'll die anyway? It's called drowning.

Then you must choose, the voice said, and Bastian was sure he'd heard a touch of humour in the voice's droned words.

Fine. I'm thinking drowning would be preferable to exploding at this stage. Bastian opened his mouth and froze in shock as he sucked in nothing but pure, clean air.

Wise choice, Sebastian Evergreen, Crown Prince of the Fae Court. Now, why do you wish to travel to Brevis?

So that was it, then? No further discussion on the near-death experience he'd just survived? Okay fine. Two could play this game. Bastian could be all business with the best of them. *I am on a quest dictated by a prophecy. It requires me to find the Oracle of the Fae to help me prevent two wrongful deaths, the outcome of which will also impact my future.*

Why do you believe the Oracle can be found on Brevis?

A Priestess from the Temple of the Fates said I would find the Oracle on Brevis. So here I am...

Very well. Your request to travel is granted. Though you may have reason to wish it had not.

What's that supposed to mean?

Bastian waited for a reply, but none came. The voice was gone. *Typical! Why did prophecies and quests always have to contain such cryptic answers or no answers at all?* Bastian had always been a fan of tasks that came with easily interpreted instructions, especially those preceded by the specific reasons and expected outcomes from the task. This blindly stumbling around getting half-answers and veiled warnings was seriously doing his head in.

His frustration faded as he considered how much worse the dragon shifter must be feeling. Jayce was doing all this without a clue about why he was doing it or what would happen if he failed or didn't try. Bastian chuckled at the thought of Jayce discovering he could be the dragon's future son-in-law. *Now, there was an interesting concept.* Bastian would be thirty-four when his fated mate turned eighteen, and Jayce would only be five years older than the man bonded to his daughter. He sure hoped the dragon shifter was open-minded enough to accept the age gap as a part of the prophecy.

Well, there was no point dwelling on what might be when nothing about the future was decided. Fates, he didn't even know if he'd survive this journey long enough to *have* a future at this stage. But then, did anyone ever really know what the Fates had in store for them? So, he needed to just suck it up and get on with it… whatever *it* turned out to be.

Danis

OKAY, so now what was supposed to happen? How long would he be required to just float in some void while holding his breath? Seriously, why were there always so many questions without any answers? Agreeing to go on a quest because some prophecy dictated that they should, when they had no idea what they were doing, bordered on insanity. Maybe he should have just listened to his gut instinct and—

Breathe, a husky male-sounding voice said in his head.

Thank the Fates was Danis' only reply. Without a second thought, he let go of the breath he'd been holding and sucked in a new one. Well, that was what the dragon shifter had told them to do, so it had to work, right?

A deep chuckle entered Danis' mind before the next

words were spoken. *Unconditional blind trust is a rare trait indeed, young Danis Farsight, Seer of the Fae Realm, and one I had thought extinct. Why do you wish to travel to Brevis?*

Well... how much time do you have? Danis waited for a reply, but none seemed forthcoming. *Okay, so the shortened version it is, then. I need to find the Oracle of the Fae to prevent a life-threatening prophecy from eventuating.*

And you were the recipient of said prophecy?

Yep.

Does the prophecy affect you or someone you love?

Well... not me personally, but I guess you could say I love the one who is affected like a brother.

Then, your request to travel is granted. And may the prophecy's new path not present too grave a burden.

Great, thanks. Wait... what? What new path? How the Fates do you know there'll be a new path? And how the Fates will I know what it is?

The silence was Danis' only reply. So, this crypticvoiced entity obviously knew way more than he was prepared to let on. *Typical.* And everything pointed to yet another hidden agenda they would have to deal with if they succeeded in their quest.

Or was this just the start of the quest? Who knew? Prophesies usually included possible outcomes if specific paths were taken. Danis would just have to hope that he would get another vision when this possible outcome changed. Seriously? What the Fates had he gotten himself into?

CHAPTER FIFTEEN

Ellie

Ellie hated it when Jayce was away overnight. Not that there had been many occasions when that actually happened. But trying to sleep alone in their big bed always had her tossing and turning for hours. And that alone was no small feat with the size of her belly. She had just drifted off into a fitful sleep when the voice started.

Mumma... can you hear me? a soft voice inside Ellie's head asked, the voice just as clear as when Jayce spoke into her mind. It had to be the voice of one of her babies. Okay, she must be dreaming. How else could one of her unborn babies be able to communicate with her already? Still, she'd play along. After all, what did she have to lose?

Yes, my darling, I can hear you.

Why are you and Daddy still angry with us?

Ellie blanched at the memory of what she'd said about them needing to stop growing. Ellie rubbed her belly, fighting back tears, hoping to soothe whatever was wrong. *Daddy and I were never angry at you, sweetheart. Why would you think we were?*

Well, we just thought it might be why we're hungry all the time now. Could we please just have a little bit more food?

Horror, fear, and a sick feeling of dread flooded Ellie's body at her baby's words. What in the Stars was going on? Why would her body not be producing enough food for the babies? Was this something to do with there being two of them to feed? No way. Lots of women carried two or more babies, and their bodies had no problem producing enough nourishment for them all.

I'm so sorry, my darling. I have no idea why this has happened. Has it been going on for long?

Since the man in the park. We think he did something bad.

Ellie woke with a start, sitting up in her lonely bed. Had it all been a dream, or had one of her baby girls just spoken to her?

Fighting back both tears and nausea, Ellie scrambled to reach her phone on her bedside table and called her mother, who picked up on the second ring.

"Ellie? What's wrong? Do you need something?" the older woman's voice sounded more alert than Ellie would have expected. But then, her mother often went without sleep for days.

"I... I..." Ellie couldn't make any words come out. She was shaking so badly she almost dropped the phone.

"I'm on my way," her mum said, and within seconds, she appeared in the doorway, rushing over to pull Ellie against her. "Stars, Elle... what's happened, honey?"

Ellie sucked in a deep breath, feeling slightly better with her mother's arms wrapped around her. "Sorry, I h-had a dream... well, I think it was a dream. But it felt so real. Oh, Mum, I don't know what to do..." Ellie trailed off as the tears slowly began to roll down her face. "What if—"

"Okay, honey," Mum said, rubbing her back and rocking them. "I need you to try to calm down so you can tell me what happened. I can't help if I don't know what's—"

"Something's wrong with the babies," Ellie cried, and she felt her mother stiffen.

"Something like what? Are you bleeding or cramping? Have the babies stopped moving? I need to know—"

"My body isn't feeding them enough. How is that even possible?"

Her mum calmly turned Ellie, so she was looking into her eyes. "Okay, Elle. Now you're frightening me. Can you at least try to explain what happened in the dream or whatever it was?"

As if just having her mother there raised her hope of finding a solution to the problem, Ellie sucked in a few calming breaths, wiped her face, and began to tell her mum what her baby had said.

When Ellie had finished speaking, she saw the panic in her mother's eyes that the older woman couldn't hide. Whether it was because Ellie had heard her unborn baby's voice or that her body wasn't functioning correctly, Ellie knew she was in trouble.

Mum stood up from the bed and started pacing around the room. Ellie could hear her muttering under her breath.

"...and of course, Jayce isn't here... something fishy about that so-called emergency meeting with the Witch Council... know what was really going on and how to get in touch with him? Rhett! Right, time to get some answers..."

Mum finally stopped pacing and faced Ellie. "Will you be okay if I just duck out for a minute? I promise not to be long."

Ellie just shrugged and looked down at her hands. "Sure... I'm not going anywhere..." and then her mother was gone.

Replaying her mum's mutterings in her mind for a few minutes, Ellie slowly worked out what the older woman obviously had. Whatever was going on, Jayce had to know more than he was saying, and had decided to keep it from Ellie so she wouldn't get upset. He'd done what he always did and gone off alone to deal with whatever situation needed handling. Something he'd promised never to do again.

She shuddered at the memories of Jayce tricking her into not following him and her mother to a meeting with a traitorous witch. That ruse had resulted in Jayce and her mum being imprisoned and tortured by Thomas Raythawn. Stars, the only reason they'd escaped was because Ellie had worked out how to syphon off some of her magic and send it to Jayce. *Seriously, would the man never learn?*

Ellie jumped when her mum popped back into the exact same space from which she'd vanished. If possible, her mother looked even worse than when she'd left.

"Okay, so tell me again what your baby girl said about the man in the park?" Mum asked before Ellie could get a word in.

"Ummm… that they think he did something bad?"

"That's what I thought. So, remember when we went to the Tree of Life for the first time, and I used a spell to check whether the entrance had been cursed?"

"Yep. From memory, Jayce was about to touch it, but you stopped him."

"Yes, that was it. Well, I'm going to use that spell on you to check whether you may have a curse on you."

"What? Are you serious?" Ellie yelled, sick of dealing with the rollercoaster of emotions she was feeling. "What if the spell hurts the babies? What if—"

"Ellie, darling. The spell is completely harmless and

unintrusive. It merely indicates whether a curse is, or has been, present. It can't remove or break it, just expose its existence."

"Fine," Ellie huffed. "Do I need to stand up?"

"No, you're fine where you are, honey. Just relax and trust me." Her mum sat down beside her and held one hand. "Okay, you ready?

Ellie nodded and held her breath.

"Contineo et Aperio Pestis." Both women's eyes went wide as what looked like a large black bruise spread across the top of the hand her mum held. A shudder ran through Ellie as she remembered her hand brushing against the old man's when they'd both reached for the dropped bag of bread.

"Stars help us," her mum finally whispered.

"Did you find out where Jayce is? I need him… right now!" Ellie growled, not sure if she wanted to scream, cry, or burst into hysterical laughter. Okay, so that last one might make her mum think she'd totally lost the plot. Which, to be honest, probably wasn't far from the truth. Ellie felt her mother's fingers brush a tear off her face. She hadn't even realised she was crying, her body too numb from shock.

"Okay honey, I need you to stay calm and listen until I'm finished… Okay?" Ellie nodded and looked into her mum's worried eyes. "I went to see Rhett. He wasn't happy about sharing what he knew, but he spilled everything once I told him about your dream."

"Apparently, some Fae prince turned up at the

Council saying he was part of a prophecy about which he couldn't share the details. Only that it involved our family's safety, and Jayce needed to go with him to Brevis to find the Oracle of the Fae. Of course, Jayce just up and followed him with no other information, not telling anyone else about it in an attempt to protect those he loves. Which we both know is typical of Jayce and what usually gets him into trouble."

"So, Jayce doesn't even know about the curse?"

"Nope. Just that his family is in danger, and he needs to fix it."

"Wait… what does any of this have to do with a Fae Prince? Hasn't the Fae realm been cut off from the other realms for like fifty years or something?"

Her mum nodded, her eyes taking on a faraway look as if she were remembering something. "Yes, it has. No one knows why they decided to shut themselves away, except that Thomas Raythawn was involved somehow."

Ellie dropped her eyes to her lap, her mind whirling from the deluge of revelations. Was it a coincidence that she'd been cursed while carrying babies believed to be descended from Thomas, the man responsible for creating a rift between the realms?

Not bloody likely! Besides, the old man who'd placed the curse on her had been on Earth. Since when were there Fae on Earth? And how the Stars could a Fae Prince be involved in a prophecy that threatened her family?

Well, one thing was for sure. Ellie knew that she and her babies had been cursed, and this Prince seemed to be the only one who knew anything useful. Fine, she knew that he couldn't share the details of the prophecy. Still, now that Ellie knew it involved her unborn babies, nothing would stop her from getting the answers needed to fix whatever was broken. Then, she would hunt down and punish the one responsible!

CHAPTER SIXTEEN

Jayce

Even though he knew what to expect from his previous experiences, Jayce still cursed as he seemed to just drop out of the bottom of the flow and land hard on his arse. He stood and rubbed his sore behind, looking around him in awe. *This* Brevis was nothing like where he'd landed on his previous visits.

Memories of Yvette's warning before they'd left for their second visit to Brevis came back to him. She'd warned them that the landscape would take on the characteristics of whatever world the visitor required.

On his first visit, he'd landed in a forest, the trees so tall he couldn't see where they ended. Home to the waters of the Living Lake, lush green grass blanketed the ground, stretching in every direction.

His second visit had been a whole different ballgame. The Book of Time had been hidden in a world of nothing but cracked, dry Earth, a barren landscape dotted with sparse and stunted plant life. Complete with a wyvern appearing in the sky, and diving to attack them only seconds after they'd arrived.

Okay, so this version of Brevis supposedly held the Oracle of the Fae, which was probably why the landscape strongly resembled pictures he'd seen in books of the Fae Realm. Maybe the old Oracle needed to be surrounded by the features of his or her native Realm. Had anyone actually mentioned whether the Oracle was a man or a woman. He couldn't remember if they had.

Remembering Bastian's parting words, Jayce pulled the seeking amulet the Fae prince had given him from his pocket. Studying the hunk of glass in his hand, he was wondering how long it would take to work when he heard a thud behind him. He whipped around, readying a power thrust against a possible threat, and found Bastian sitting on the ground and looking around with a look of disgust on his face.

"What the Fates is going on? Why would that Aqueous Flow thing tell me I was going to Brevis and then toss me back out in the Fae Realm?" Bastian stood and brushed off his pants. Then, as if noticing Jayce for the first time, he scratched his head, the look of disgust changing to one of confusion. "Wait... what are you doing here? You're supposed to be on Brevis."

Jayce threw back his head and roared with laughter.

Wow, the landscape must be a dead ringer for that of the Fae realm if Bastian thought he was back there.

"What the Fates are you laughing at?" Bastian huffed, folding his arms in front of his chest. "Did I miss something?"

"Sorry, man," Jayce spluttered, trying to rein in his laughter. "It's just that I *am* on Brevis… and so are *you*. I guess no one told you that Brevis is ever-changing, evolving into different landscapes to serve the needs of whatever or whomever you seek. So, this is really what the Fae realm looks like? I gotta say, it's pretty impressive."

Bastian stood and looked around with a stunned expression. "This is incredible. It's like a mirror image of my home. But the Fae Realm is huge. How are we supposed to find the Oracle? He could be—"

A familiar thud sounded behind Jayce, and he again prepared for an attack. Then he smiled as he turned to find another dazed young fae sitting on the ground in stunned silence.

Now, it was Bastian's turn to laugh at the expression on his friend's face. "Okay…" he spluttered at Jayce. "Jayce, meet my best friend, Danis. Now I see why you couldn't help laughing. Did I look like that?"

Jayce chuckled. "Pretty close. Although you looked more disgusted than stunned. But it wasn't until you spoke that I couldn't hold back the laugh."

Danis growled from where he sat, and Jayce and

Bastian instantly sobered. "What the Fates is going on? Why are we—"

Bastian held up his hand and moved to help his friend to his feet. "Before you end up sounding as stupid as I did, we *are* on Brevis. It's just a mirror image of our homeland."

Danis looked from Bastian to Jayce as if trying to work out if they were joking. "No way. I mean… look at it! And I can even see the palace spires over there. How the Fates could this even be possible?"

Jayce just shrugged at the young fae's question. "Nice to meet you Danis. Yeah, that's something Brevis tends to do. Once you tell the voice inside the flow what you are seeking, the landscape becomes whatever it needs to be to accommodate your request. I'm sure we'll find out soon enough why we appear to be in the fae Realm.

As he spoke, Jayce took in their surroundings in further detail. They appeared to have landed in a meadow covered in lush green grass, with wildflowers growing at random every few paces. As Danis had said, there were spires in the distance, and Jayce knew instinctively that was where they needed to go.

When he found nowhere suitable to discuss their situation, he fetched the table and chairs from the small room where he'd met Bastian earlier that day. He was relieved to confirm that what Ellie had said about being able to fetch from other realms also applied to

Brevis. He grinned as the two Fae just stared from Jayce to the furniture he'd fetched and back.

"What the—?" Bastian spluttered.

"How did—?" Danis said at the same time.

"Oh, did I forget to tell you boys I have magic? Sorry about that. Must have slipped my mind in all the rushing around."

"But dragons don't have magic," Bastian replied, eyeing Jayce with a wary look. "How is it that you do?"

Jayce smiled and sat down on one of the chairs he'd fetched. "Please, why don't we all sit? It sounds like it might be time for us all to share a few secrets."

He watched as Bastian and Danis looked at each other, then pulled out chairs and sat at the table. Jayce then fetched three bottles of water from the fridge back in his office and leaned back in his chair. "Okay, so I'm happy to start. I'll try to give you the shortened version of how I acquired my own magic."

Bastian

BASTIAN SHOOK his head and tried to absorb everything the dragon shifter had told them. It had to be the truth because nobody could make up a story like the one he'd just heard! Details of forbidden bonds, never-before-seen powers and insanity averted had the prince's head spinning. He suddenly felt very young and inexperienced in front of this god-like man.

"Wow. My life has been so uneventful compared to yours. I've basically just spent my whole life pampered and protected while living in a palace. I don't even know what made me think I was capable of doing whatever it is we need to do," Bastian said, feeling like a complete fraud.

"Hey," Jayce said with a smile. "You guys are only what? Sixteen? At your age, I was still partying and going to school. Don't go beating yourself up just yet."

"But she's my fated mate. I need to—" Bastian broke off in horror. What the Fates had made that slip out? He wasn't supposed to reveal anything about the prophecy. And by the look on Jayce's face, he knew he was in big trouble.

"Who. Is. Your. Fated. Mate?" Jayce growled, and Bastian didn't know whether to run or curl up into a ball. What was he supposed to do now, for fate's sake?

"Well…ummm… I can't… the prophecy…"

"I don't give a shit what the rules are about prophecies. You are going to tell me everything you know, and it better be right now."

"Ummm, sorry to interrupt," Danis said in a slightly shaky voice. "But I'm the one who had the vision regarding the prophecy. It was very specific about the necessity of your involvement in whatever it is we have to do, but that the details must not be revealed in order to convince you to help us. It had to be your choice to join us."

"Yeah… what he said," Bastian added, feeling slightly braver after his friend's defensive words. "Plus, the old Priestess said the same."

"I don't suppose anyone mentioned the penalty if the rules were broken?" Jayce growled. "Because, in my experience, nothing could be as bad as what I want to do right now if you don't tell me."

Danis stood up and threw his hands in the air. "Fine. If you want to risk the repercussions of not doing what the vision dictated, so be it. But as a Seer, I'm invoking plausible deniability. I'll be over by that tree when you're ready to get back to planning what we should do next." Danis headed for the tree without another word or a backward glance.

"Fine. But knowing the stakes and what the prophecy revealed, how do we know that breaking the rules won't make things worse for those already affected?" Bastian asked, trying to impress upon Jayce all the possible risks of revealing the details of the prophecy.

"I know, I know," Jayce said, standing and pacing as he ran his hands through his hair. "I've had plenty of experience with prophecies. I know their secrets are always closely guarded. But there is sometimes a loophole. What was the exact wording in the vision? Did Danis tell you?"

Bastian thought back to the conversation where

Danis had told him about his vision, and excitement began to run through his veins. "Wait, he said we weren't allowed to tell you the details while trying to convince you to join us. But there was nothing about not telling you once we were on our way." He turned and yelled toward his friend standing near the tree. "Danis? We need you to come and verify some details from the vision. It's okay, we haven't broken any rules yet."

Danis shrugged and headed back to the table. "What? I've already told you I'm not—"

"Oh, cut the crap, Danis. Just listen, will you? Did the vision only say that we couldn't tell Jayce the details of the prophecy while convincing him to help us? Nothing about after he agreed to help, and we were on our way?"

Danis' eyes widened, and the smile Bastian was used to seeing on his friend's face reappeared. "Well, Fates be damned! You're right. We just completely misinterpreted the warning." He turned to smile at Jayce. "Maybe we should all sit back down first. I'm thinking there might be a few details you'll struggle to wrap your head around."

CHAPTER SEVENTEEN

Ellie

"I'm sorry, Mother," Ellie said through gritted teeth, wringing her hands as she paced the room. "There is nothing you can say that will stop me from going to Brevis. So, you can either accompany me to the Aqueous Flow entrance in the Witch Realm or stay here and wait for me to come back."

Ellie couldn't believe her mother still thought she could talk her strong-willed—*okay, so maybe stubborn was a more apt description*—daughter out of doing anything she set her heart on. Okay, so Ellie knew that travelling through the Aqueous Flow while pregnant might not be the best idea she'd ever had, but the threat to her babies' lives if she did nothing was far greater.

Besides, she couldn't deal with any of this without Jayce by her side.

"Fine. I'll come to the Witch Realm with you, but can we at least wait until daylight? Nothing good will come from forcing our way into the Witch's Council rooms in the middle of the night."

Ellie slumped back down onto her bed, cradling her swollen belly in her arms. "Why is this happening to us? What if I can't save them? What if—"

Ellie's mum sat behind her on the bed and rubbed her aching shoulders, something her mother always seemed to know when she needed. "Deep breaths, honey. Everything is going to be fine. Rhett said the Fae Prince seemed like a decent young man and genuinely wanted to help us. Although, he wouldn't tell Jayce why he needed to help or what he would get if they succeeded. Still, beggars can't be choosers, and I have a feeling we'll need the Fae's help if a prophecy is involved."

ELLIE BLINKED and looked around in surprise after her mum teleported them to the Witch Realm. She hadn't thought to specify where exactly she wanted to arrive in the realm, so she shouldn't have been surprised to find them inside her mother's home. Ellie had only ever been there a couple of times over the years, and still never failed to be surprised to find herself standing in an exact replica of her Aunt Serena and Emelda's home on Earth. The same home in which Ellie had lived for almost eighteen years, believing her mother dead.

Ellie snapped out of her memories as her mum wrapped an arm around her waist. Or at least she tried. The mammoth task of anyone succeeding in that endeavour almost made her laugh. *Almost.* Somehow, laughter had become a luxury she couldn't quite achieve right then.

"Have I told you lately how proud I am of you?" Her mum said, sadness and worry in her eyes. "I feel like the luckiest mother and soon-to-be grandmother ever born." She sighed and removed her arm from Ellie's waist. "Which is why I hate the thought of you and my unborn granddaughters going to Brevis alone. I couldn't bear the thought of losing—"

Ellie enveloped her mother in a warm hug. "Don't stress. We'll be fine. You'll be there with me right up until I enter the pool, and we know Jayce will be at the other end. Once we're back in the same realm, I'll be able to contact him through our bond. What could possibly go wrong?"

Her mother took both of Ellie's hands in hers, and they stood looking at each other. "Just promise me you'll be careful. Don't do anything to put you or the babies at risk. You need to come straight back if there's any sign of danger. Okay?"

Ellie squeezed her mother's hands and nodded. "I promise. Now, can we please get going? I just want this whole thing over with."

Her mother grinned. "Not to mention you're missing Jayce already, hmmm?"

Ellie chuckled and rubbed her belly. "Maybe we all are..." Ellie mumbled as they headed out the door.

The walk to the Witch's Council was totally different to the first time they'd strolled down the street arm in arm, when the few people they encountered had gone out of their way to avoid making eye contact. This time, people called out greetings as they passed, commenting on the progression of Ellie's pregnancy and wishing them luck and good fortune.

Wow, how things had changed. Ellie remembered cowering behind her mother, under a glamour to appear as an old woman. Yeah, having a death warrant hanging over your head could really make things difficult. Still, it was better than carrying two babies in a body that had been cursed.

Ellie's morbid thoughts were cut off as they reached the entrance to the Witch's Council. Mum had told Helena to expect them, explaining to the Head witch that Ellie needed to travel to Brevis to see Jayce urgently. Helena had looked surprised to hear that

Jayce was on Brevis but said nothing. Her mother had told her long ago that Helena had nothing but respect for Jayce and Ellie for their past sacrifices to save the realms. The old witch would never question their need for anything.

"Stars above Ellie, look at you," the old witch said with a smile. "You know, I wasn't even surprised when I heard you were expecting twins. After all, you and Jayce are renowned for achieving the impossible. The rarity of conceiving twins was to be expected when the Stars have favoured both parents."

Ellie smiled, trying not to laugh at the pride oozing from her mother's pores. Her puffed-out chest and regal stance were just so cute.

"Yes, we are indeed blessed," her mother replied. But then, as if reality had broken through her happiness bubble, her shoulders slumped, and her face paled. "I'm sorry, Helena, but Ellie needs to get going. Maybe we can catch up over coffee after I see her off?"

"Of course," Helena said, frowning at her mum's complete change in demeanour. "You know the way. I'll be in my office if you need me. Safe travels, Ellie."

Ellie didn't miss the way Helena's eyes flicked down to her massive belly before looking away. Of course, the older woman would consider her a fool for travelling in the Aqueous Flow when she was so very pregnant. But what Helena, or anyone else, thought didn't matter. Ellie could live with being judged a thousand times over if it meant her babies would be safe.

Her mother must have seen the judgmental look, too, as she silently grasped Ellie's hand in hers, and they headed for the pool that led to Brevis. Nausea rose in Ellie's throat as memories of the previous times she'd travelled in the Aqueous Flow flooded in. Sucking in a deep breath, she pushed the nausea and the memories aside, determined to just get to Jayce before she dropped her bundle and turned into a blithering idiot.

Pushing the door to the meeting room open, Ellie and her mum stepped through and hurried to the small alcove where they knew the pool sat.

"You okay, sweetheart?" her mum whispered, squeezing her hand.

"Yep… well, not really, but I have to be, don't I?" Ellie replied softly. She had no idea why they were whispering, but it seemed appropriate in the vast hall surrounding them.

"Oh, honey, I wish I could fix this or at least do it for you. I don't understand how the Stars can allow this to happen to you after everything you and Jayce have already been through."

Ellie squeezed her mother's hand one more time, then dropped it and tried to step up onto the lip of the pool. Unfortunately, what had been a simple task the last time she'd been here was now made impossible by her huge stomach throwing off her natural balance. "Yeah, maybe I won't be diving into the pool this time. If I sit on the edge, can you please help me swing my legs over so I can just slither in, kinda like a beached whale?"

She finally met her mother's eyes, and they began to giggle at the absurdity of their entire situation. Seriously? Ellie couldn't even get into the pool without help, and here she was, thinking she was off to kick arse like she had in the old days. Well, at least her magic was still intact.

Suddenly, her giggles evaporated when she remembered her magic doing that weird explosion thing before any of this started. Stars, what if her magic went haywire when she needed it?

Oh, for Star's sake! She needed the words 'what if' erased from her vocabulary. They only ever made things worse.

Her mum had helped Ellie move into position on the pool's edge while they giggled, only to freeze when she noticed Ellie's worried frown. "What's wrong? Have you changed your mind? Because we can turn around and go back home—"

Ellie shook her head and tried to paste a smile back onto her face. There was no way she would remind her mother of the magical malfunction she'd had the other day. Her mum would never let her go if she thought for one minute that Ellie might be defenceless in a place like Brevis. "No, Mum, I'm fine. Some of the less pleasant memories of travelling in the flow just sneaked up on me. But I've sent them packing, and I'm ready to go. I love you."

"I love you too, sweetheart," her mum said, her eyes glassy with unshed tears. "Now stop talking and go find your man."

Too choked with emotion to speak, Ellie simply nodded and slipped into the cool, calm waters of the Aqueous Flow.

CHAPTER EIGHTEEN

Jayce

By the time Danis had finished explaining the details of the prophecy, Jayce wasn't sure whether his head or his heart would explode first. Some sick bastard had put a curse on Ellie, and it was killing their babies? Pushing his chair back from the table, he stood and let out a bellowing roar.

He couldn't believe that, even from the grave, the evil that was Thomas Raythawn could still destroy Jayce and his family's lives. Unfortunately, many of the inhabitants of the various worlds still believed Thomas had been his biological father. Hell, Jayce had only learned that he *wasn't* shortly before he and Ellie had ended the maniac's life.

As for the other revelation from the prophecy, the

one where his sixteen-year-old fae companion Sebastian Evergreen, the Prince of the Spring Court, was his unborn daughter's fated mate? Yeah, he'd deal with that elephant-in-the-room when his head wasn't quite so volatile.

When he realised the two fae teens sat cowering in fear at his explosive reaction, Jayce sucked in a deep breath and tried to get his emotions back under control. Okay, so maybe being this close to a furious man who could turn into a dragon and burn them alive might present a scary prospect. Especially when they didn't even know him, or that he would never do something like that.

"Sorry, boys. I know this isn't your fault. I just needed to vent for a minute. Don't worry, I have no intention of killing the messenger, as they say."

Bastian seemed to recover first and attempted to paste what Jayce assumed was meant to be a smile onto his ghostly white face. "I'm so sorry, Jayce. I can't even imagine how you must be feeling right now. But at least now you understand the gravity of the situation. We don't know much about the curse, except that it works by twisting the mother's brain into believing she is no longer pregnant, so her body will stop feeding the babies. But we don't know its strength or how fast it works."

Jayce groaned and covered his face with his hands. "Stars help us! This explains the headaches Ellie has been fighting. Her brain is at war against accepting and implementing the curse. If anyone can fight against it, Ellie can. She's the strongest person I've ever met, not to mention the most stubborn. This curse will have its work cut out for it trying to convince *that* brain to give in."

Danis finally seemed to have recovered from Jayce's outburst as he sat up a bit straighter and sighed. "Well, that's awesome news. At least we know that it hadn't taken over before you left. Let's just hope she can buy us a little more time so we can find the Oracle and get the damn cure."

"Ummm… so Jayce… about—" Bastian had gone from ghostly white to beetroot red in the blink of an eye.

Jayce held up his hand and gave Bastian a stern look he tried to temper with empathy. "No, Bastian. We will definitely not be discussing the other matter until this curse is removed. But once again, I have to say that I know none of this is your fault and will try to focus on that fact until this is over."

Bastian

BASTIAN SAGGED with relief at the dragon shifter's words. For a minute there, he'd thought both he and Danis would end up as crispy critters before their search had even begun. Not that he blamed Jayce for reacting the way he had. But there was a vast difference between a normal man losing his temper and a dragon shifter dealing with the same problem.

"Well, I'm thinking we'd best start searching for this Oracle," Danis said, ever the voice of reason. "By my calculations, it would be almost morning in the dragon realm. It's time we did something about helping Ellie fight these headaches and get her the cure. Not to mention making sure those precious babies continue to get enough to eat."

Bastian smiled at Danis and grabbed his friend's shoulder. "You are so right, my friend. I say we head toward the palace spires and see what we can find. I reckon the Oracle is sure to be somewhere inside that place. What do you guys think?"

"Yeah, you're probably right. But even if the Oracle isn't there, there might be some clue about how or where to find him," Danis replied.

"Great. Then, let's get moving. Time's a-wastin', and I need to get home to my wife," Jayce said as the table and chairs vanished, only to be replaced by three heavily stuffed backpacks.

Bastian looked from the meagre backpack he'd brought with him to the one Jayce was offering him.

No question there which one he'd choose. He looked over at Danis to find him rifling through the backpack he'd brought with him, pulling out a few items and stuffing them into the one provided by Jayce.

Bastian smiled as he proceeded to copy his friend's actions. Of course Danis would think to grab the important stuff they'd brought from home. Within a few minutes, the two fae boys had tucked their own backpacks away behind some trees, thanking Jayce and shouldering the ones he'd supplied.

Jayce chuckled as he threw his own over his shoulder and began to walk towards the palace spire in the distance. "Never hurts to be prepared."

Bastian adjusted the heavy backpack on his shoulders and followed Jayce. He couldn't help admiring the other man's ability to compartmentalise his emotions in order to get the job done. *Fates!* Jayce was only five years older than him, yet the dragon shifter made Bastian feel like a small child.

Okay, so Bastian knew that Jayce's life experiences had played a large part in making the dragon shifter into the fiercely loyal and determined man he was today. Bastian could only hope to eventually learn to emulate the other man's enviable qualities. Oh, and he'd really like that to be sooner rather than later.

Ellie

CALMLY HOLDING her breath and waiting for the familiar voice inside the Aqueous Flow, Ellie tried to formulate a plan to ensure she was dropped in exactly the same place Jayce had been. She didn't want either of them to waste time searching for each other. Yes, they could speak to each other in their minds, but that didn't help if they were on opposite sides of whatever world they landed in.

Breathe... the voice said, and Ellie didn't even hesitate. Her days of questioning and arguing over everything were a thing of the past. These days, she made decisions based on what would be best for her family. And right now, breathing was at the top of that list.

Aah... Daughter of the Stars. I see you have not come alone this time.

Ellie actually found herself looking around for the other person the voice had referred to. Then his meaning dawned on her, and she giggled, rubbing her belly to ensure her babies stayed calm.

Oh... yes. I'm afraid it was impossible to leave them behind... literally.

Of course. And why do you wish to travel to Brevis this time?

I need to find Jayce, and I know that's where he is.

Does your need involve the curse you currently carry?

Of course, he would be able to detect the curse. He always seemed to know everything about everybody.

It does, she replied. *If not removed, the curse will kill my babies.*

I understand the urgency and will grant your wish to travel. I will also ensure you arrive at the same place where your husband was delivered.

Ellie bit back the tears threatening to escape at the voice's kindness. It was an emotion she hadn't thought the entity capable of. But then, maybe he didn't get a lot of repeat customers. She laughed at herself for even attempting to analyse the workings of an entity that consisted of nothing more than a voice.

She hoped Jayce hadn't moved too far from where the Aqueous had dropped him. She could only guess how long he'd already been there without knowing exactly what time he'd left the previous night. Still, it hadn't been more than twelve hours since she'd last seen him, so hopefully, he hadn't been on Brevis too long.

Ellie was surprised when she felt her body being lifted up, only to descend from the flow and be paced gently on the hard ground below. Wow! The other times she'd travelled, there'd been a sudden drop and then a thud as she hit the ground. Apparently, the voice hadn't wanted the babies hurt and had supported her landing. *Who'd have ever guessed the old entity had it in him?*

She looked around at where she'd landed and could tell from the indents in the lush green grass that someone had been there recently. Now, she just needed to make sure the who and the when were the right ones.

Jayce? she said in her mind. *Where are you, baby? I need you.*

Ellie? How the hell...? Are you seriously here on Brevis? Why would you risk coming here? The babies—

Are dying, Jayce. They told me they were hungry—

What? How... wait. Do you even know where you are?

The voice in the Aqueous promised he'd drop me exactly where he dropped you. I can see from the disturbed grass that someone was—

Okay, stay exactly where you are. I'm not too far away, and I'm coming right now.

Ellie sunk to the ground in relief. At least she'd found Jayce. Now, she wouldn't have to deal with everything on her own. She still found it hard to believe how much she relied on Jayce. She could remember a time when she'd been so independent and determined not to rely on anyone else. Well, that had been when she only had her own well-being to consider. Now that she had two other beings growing inside her, she was happy to take all the help and support she could get.

It had only been a few minutes before the sound of wings flapping told her Jayce was close. Knowing he was close, a euphoric sense of peace descended over her for the first time since she'd heard her baby's voice inside her head. Ellie looked up to see her man in his magnificent dragon form carrying two men on his back.

Hmmm… it looked like *someone* had quite a bit of explaining to do.

CHAPTER NINETEEN

Jayce

*J*ayce? *Where are you, baby? I need you.*

When Ellie's voice entered his mind, Jayce had almost jumped out of his skin. He knew their telepathic ability didn't work when they were in separate worlds. So how…?

By the time Ellie had explained why she was on Brevis, his heart was thumping like a jackhammer. Turning to where Bastian and Danis stood staring at him, wondering why he looked so panicked, he didn't waste words. "Okay, boys. You're about to get your very first dragon ride. Ellie is here on Brevis, and I need to get to her. I haven't got time to answer any questions right now, but just know that once I morph, you'll need to get on. I'll swing my tail around, and you can use it to get onto my back. Then, hold on until you see a very pregnant woman on the ground below us and wait for me to land. You can use my tail again to get off."

"But how—" Bastian started.

"I don't know—" Danis said at the same time.

Jayce's snarl cut them both off. He hadn't meant to scare them, but he didn't want Ellie and the babies alone in this foreign world for longer than he could help. Bastian and Danis were suddenly both nodding, and he smiled. "Thanks, guys. I knew you'd be up for it."

Without another word, he turned and walked far enough away that he wouldn't squash them when his Dragon emerged. If he weren't so desperate to get to Ellie, Jayce would have enjoyed watching the two fae boys' shocked expressions as he grew into his massive Dragon.

Jayce had to admit he was proud of them when they climbed onto his tail, and then his back, with little hesitation. When he felt all movement on his back cease, Jayce assumed they were ready to go and launched himself into the air.

The three of them had only been walking for a couple of hours, so he knew reaching Ellie wouldn't take long. Knowing the animosity the fae felt against dragons, he hadn't wanted to risk being exposed. But this was for Ellie, and nothing else mattered.

Within minutes, Jayce caught sight of Ellie sitting in the lush grass, her head tipped back to catch the sun and looking as if she didn't have a care in the world. She was so beautiful that it made his heart ache. How could the Stars allow this to happen to such a loving, giving woman like Ellie? She'd always done everything they asked of her and more, and this was how they repaid her? Yeah, someone up there was just begging to get an arse-kicking from a very angry dragon. And if they couldn't get the curse lifted…?

Jayce snapped himself out of his angry thoughts and stretched out his talons to land. As soon as he was on the ground, he felt the movement of the two boys and brought his tail around to help them down. As soon as they were safely off, he morphed back to his human form.

"Fates Jayce. That was… well… indescribable," Bastian gushed as soon as he hit the ground.

"That was seriously the most amazing experience of my entire life," Danis babbled, bouncing on his feet as if he had ants in his pants.

"I'd recommend you reel in some of that enthusiasm, boys. I have a feeling we are in a helluva lot of trouble," he indicated over their shoulders to where Ellie was marching towards them with that *you-are-dead-meat-Jayce-Raythawn* look he hadn't seen in a while.

"Don't you even think about being angry with me for coming to Brevis, Mr Liar-liar-pants-on-fire Jayce Raythawn. Mind telling me where the members of the Witch Council you came to meet are hiding?"

Jayce didn't even bother to respond. Instead, he moved toward her and pulled her into his arms. He sighed in relief when her hands moved up and behind his head.

"I'm so sorry, sweetheart. I have no idea how much you know, or even how you could know anything, but I think it might be best if we all sit and discuss the situation and where to go from here."

"Well, only if it doesn't take too long. I have no idea how long we have until…" Then she burst into tears and slumped in his arms. He seriously should have known better than to keep any of this from her. But he'd never imagined she might find out what was happening when he wasn't there and be left to deal with it alone.

As for *how* she'd found out. Had she really said the babies told her they were hungry? Not that he should have been surprised. He'd already suspected they would be incredibly powerful, considering their lineage. So, of course, one of their six-month-old unborn foetuses could communicate with her mother's mind. After all, hadn't he and Ellie always been told that what they could do should be impossible? Obviously, their babies were already chips-off-the-old-block.

Bastian

BASTIAN COULDN'T TAKE his eyes off the stunningly beautiful woman Jayce held in his arms. Wow, if her daughters grew up to be even half as lovely as her, they would be stunners.

"Just wow, man," Danis whispered beside him. "I'm thinking your fated mate comes from some incredibly good genes. Fates, I'm totally jealous right now."

Bastian clapped his hand on his friend's back. "And if it wasn't for you, I might never have known I even had a fated mate." He shuddered as his own words reinforced the urgency of their mission. Looking over at Jayce and Ellie sitting on the grass with their heads together, Bastian moved to sit opposite them and cleared his throat.

"Please excuse me for interrupting your reunion, but time isn't something we have a lot of right now." He didn't miss the curiosity burning in Ellie's eyes, and he knew Jayce hadn't even begun to explain what was going on. "It is an honour to meet you, Ellie Raythawn. My name is Sebastian Evergreen, Crown Prince of the Spring Court in the Fae Realm, and this is my friend Danis Farsight. Perhaps it would be best if Danis, the seer who received the details of the prophecy, shared everything he learned in his vision. Then you can ask any questions you may have when he's finished?"

Ellie looked into Bastian's eyes as if she were trying to read where he fit into all this. Well, she'd know soon enough. He could only hope she took the news about him being her future son-in-law better than Jayce had.

Bastian watched the myriad of expressions flitting across Ellie's expressive face as she listened to Danis repeat the details of his vision exactly as Bastian had already heard twice before. As he'd anticipated, her eyes flew to his when she learned that Bastian was the fated mate of one of her unborn babies. What did surprise him was the speculative look that grew in those expressive eyes.

An uncomfortable silence hung in the air when Danis finished speaking. Bastian figured everyone was busy absorbing the details of the horrific events that had led to them all sitting here in this alien world.

"Prince Sebastian, can I ask how old you are?" Ellie asked, breaking the silence while maintaining the speculative look.

"Please, my friends call me Bastian. And I am sixteen years old. I know the age—" he started, only to be interrupted when Ellie held up her hand.

"It's okay, Bastian. Who are we to question what has obviously been pre-ordained for a very long time? Ask Jayce for the details of how we met if you think this is weird." Ellie giggled and gave Jayce a cheeky smile, who just groaned and pulled her closer against him.

"Fate is not something easily changed or messed with," Ellie continued. "Which is why what we have to accomplish here might end up messy and not without sacrifice. But I refuse to accept the cruel fate destined for my babies, and I will do anything to change it. Because, let's face it, unless we can succeed in reversing the first part, the second part has no hope of ever coming true."

Bastian's heart clenched at the reality of what Ellie had just said. Like Ellie, he refused to accept the possibility of failure and its devastating impact on his own future. But he also felt an incredible amount of empathy for these two people who'd done so much for others and been repaid with this horrific situation. Bastian looked from Ellie to Jayce and then back to Ellie, a fierce determination rising in his chest. "I agree. Failure is not an option."

Ellie smiled as she rubbed her belly. "Well, whatever your reasons for offering to help, we can't thank you enough for what you're doing."

"When Danis first told me about the vision he'd had, I was horrified by what had been done to you and the babies. Sure, the fact that one of those babies might end up being my fated mate played a part in my decision. But I just turned sixteen and am a long way from even considering that kind of stuff. So whether or not that factor comes into play in the distant future, I'm somehow needed in the curse-breaking process."

Bastian sucked in a breath and continued. "So here we all are, and if it's okay with you, I'd rather leave the whole fated mate scenario out of the equation for now. I'd much rather envisage my fated mate as a beautiful, full-grown woman than an unborn baby."

"I can definitely understand that. And to be honest, I'd be more than relieved to have any thoughts of my unborn child mated to my sixteen-year-old travel companion permanently erased from my brain," Jayce replied, smiling at Ellie.

CHAPTER TWENTY

Danis

Danis was so proud of his best friend and the way he was dealing with the shitshow ahead of them. He'd often worried that Bastian acted way too emotionless and shallow when faced with a dilemma, but he now saw that for what it was. Those occasions were merely Bastian emulating his father, the king's, predominantly heartless and dismissive behaviour. The real Bastian, the one standing here promising to help two strangers rectify a wrong, was the one he loved like a brother. The man who would one day make an amazing king.

But pushing all the emotional declarations aside, it was time for someone to step up and be the voice of reason. Because every minute they sat here increased the risk of their possible failure.

"Okay, people, sorry to have to be the voice of logic here, but we are wasting precious time we don't have. Ellie, how are the headaches?" Danis asked as if he were enquiring about the weather.

Ellie's face paled, lifting a hand to her face. "Oh, Stars, Jayce. The headaches have been getting less intense. Does that mean my brain's stopped fighting the curse?"

Jayce's face paled to match his wife's, and Danis knew without a doubt that it was time for an intervention. Understanding that the three white-faced, over-emotional people would be incapable of making rational decisions, Danis leapt into gear.

"Right, time to get moving then. I don't know if Jayce told you, Ellie, but this version of Brevis appears to be an exact replica of our home, the Fae realm. We were headed towards the spires in the distance when you arrived. We figure the castle is as good a place as any to start looking for the Oracle."

The feel of Bastian squeezing his shoulder told Danis he appreciated his friend's stoic handling of the situation. They all rose, and Danis was relieved to see the determination back on their faces. Now maybe, they might get some shit done.

"So... can I assume travelling by dragon isn't an option?" Ellie asked as they picked up their packs and headed off.

"You assume correctly, baby. We have no idea what to expect in this world, but dragons haven't been welcome in the Fae realm for quite some time. I only risked it because I was in a hurry to get to you."

Ellie just nodded and squared her shoulders, but Danis didn't miss the disappointment that crossed her face. He suspected that Ellie was nowhere near as unaffected by the curse as she'd have them believe.

They'd been walking at a good pace for at least four hours when they caught sight of the first outlying house, which Danis knew signified the start of the village surrounding the castle. As they drew closer, he was relieved to see the usual townsfolk milling about in the square.

He'd been worried that this version of the Fae realm may have been uninhabited. At least now they'd be able to ask if anyone knew the whereabouts of the Oracle. But the closer they got to the bustling little village, the more confused Danis felt. Not one person had even looked their way, a relatively unheard-of response to the arrival of strangers.

Shrugging, he was headed toward a man sitting on a bench with a metal tankard to his lips when Bastian pulled him back and turned Danis to face him. "Danis? Don't you think it's a bit strange that no one has even acknowledged our presence yet?" Bastian said quietly, sporting a worried frown.

"Hey, boys," Jayce said, stopping when he stood beside them. "Am I imagining things, or is something weird going on here? Like maybe no one can see us?"

Raising his fingers to his mouth, Danis blew out a

deafening whistle. They watched dumbstruck as no one turned their head in response to the sound. "Yep, something's weird, all right. They can't see or hear us. Now, what the hell are we supposed to do?"

"Well, we can see and hear them, so I'm thinking we walk around and do some eavesdropping. There's bound to be someone gossiping about the goings-on in the palace," Bastian said, pointing toward two women chatting on the street.

"Of course," Danis said, and when he caught sight of a couple of palace guards, his spirits lifted. "And who better to listen in on than a couple of palace guards? I've lost count of the number of times I've heard them bellyaching about how hard they work for so little pay while the aristocrats gallivant around and do as they please."

"Okay, so we split up and call out if anyone hears anything useful. Everyone good with that?"

They all nodded, and Danis made a beeline for the guards he'd spotted earlier. He'd been listening to their boring conversation for about ten minutes and was just about to give up and walk away when the conversation took an interesting turn.

"Some people are saying it might be time to reinstate the Kings of the Fae Courts," the first guard said, and his words instantly pulled Danis' attention. "It's been centuries since the War of the Kings. Surely none of their surviving ancestors would let it happen again." Wait... no monarchy and a war between the kings? What the hell had happened in this alternate world?

"Exactly. Everyone knows the current members of the Fae Council are a bunch of money-grubbing, power-hungry scumbags," the second guard said, scratching his bushy beard. "I don't understand why the old man puts up with their political shenanigans. But then again, he's been in the public eye less and less over the past few years. Most of the time, he locks himself away in that decrepit old suite in which the royals used to live. Maybe he's just too old to care any longer. I mean, he must be ancient, right?"

"Yeah, true. But I'm pretty sure the old dude's immortal, so age shouldn't even come into it. I used to think it would be so cool to live forever, but after watching how little interaction he has with anyone, I reckon it would be a sad, lonely old life. Nope, he may be all-knowing, all-seeing, and around until the end of eternity, but there's no way I'd ever wanna do his job. I mean, it's not like he can just say 'Thanks, but I don't wanna be the Oracle anymore. Give someone else a turn'."

Danis hadn't even realised he'd been holding his breath until the two men chuckled and moved on to a new topic. Releasing the breath, he sucked in new ones as if his life depended on it. Hey, it just might. He must have been close to passing out from lack of oxygen.

He looked around him and decided against searching for the others. Instead, he grinned and once again blew a deafening whistle. As he'd expected, the other three were there in under a minute. And then everyone was speaking at once.

"Did you hear something—" Bastian.

"That bloody whistle—" Jayce.

"Please tell me you—" Ellie.

Danis held his fingers up to his lips as if he were going to whistle again, and everyone instantly stopped talking.

"Much better. Now, if you can all keep quiet, I'll tell you about the bizarre conversation I just overheard."

By the time Danis had finished relating everything he'd heard, a stunned silence had fallen over the group.

"What in all the Fates was the War of the Kings?" Bastian asked quietly, his face ashen. "And is this world really just an alternate to ours, or is it the future of the Fae Realm?"

Danis squeezed his friend's shoulder and spoke to the group. "I think we all know we won't find the answers until we locate the Oracle. Lucky for us, Bastian and I know everything there is to know about the castle's layout. But I have absolutely no idea how to break into a castle." He looked over at Jayce and Ellie with a wicked grin. "Although something tells me you two would be experts at this type of thing. Which means it's your turn to take the lead, I reckon."

CHAPTER TWENTY-ONE

Jayce

*J*ayce tried to quell the old thrill of excitement at the chance to practice some of the skills they'd acquired back when they were on the run. And when he glanced at Ellie, it was clear she shared that same feeling. After Thomas' passing, they'd been so sick of the constant need to flee, conceal themselves, and battle for their lives, that they'd gladly stepped away. Still, the exhilarating memories of feeling like a hero sometimes resonated in his mind.

"I know what you're thinking, baby," Ellie said, weaving the fingers of her hand with his. "I miss it too, sometimes. But I love our lives without all that even more."

Jayce pulled Ellie into his arms, brushing his lips

softly over her forehead. Ellie was right. He wouldn't trade what they had now for anything, especially since he'd started delegating some of his Council responsibilities. He planned to spend as much time with Ellie as possible before the babies were born. And after they were born...

The sobering thought pulled his stupid daydreaming head out of the clouds and back to reality. They needed to formulate a plan to get to the Oracle and find out how to neutralise the curse. Ellie's brain was slowly losing the battle against the curse's intrusion, and they were running out of time.

"Well, Danis is right that it wouldn't be the first time Ellie and I have had to break in somewhere, but doing it while invisible is a whole different ball game. We'll have to find a way to get others to open doors and to leave that door open behind them, all while thinking it was their own idea to do it. Does anyone have any thoughts?"

Ellie's face broke into that wicked smile Jayce knew so well. She stooped and picked up a stone off the ground, tossing it in her hand and looking around. Then she threw the stone at the metal tankard now sitting on the bench beside the man who'd been drinking from it. The loud clang and the way the man jumped up when the tankard flew back against the wall were priceless.

"Seems they may not be able to see or hear us, but we can still affect their surroundings. So we shouldn't have any trouble opening doors. Oooh… this is starting to feel like old times," Ellie said, throwing her arms around Jayce's neck. So, of course, he had to reward his clever little minx with a kiss. What else could a man do, right?

Jayce became aware of Bastian clearing his throat and quickly broke the searing kiss with his beautiful wife. He'd almost forgotten they were in public, and his face burned at the curious look in both boys' eyes.

"Don't even think about judging. I'm sure it won't be too long before—" Ellie said, smiling at the two boys' quickly reddening cheeks.

"O-kay," Jayce interjected. He hadn't missed the signs of fatigue his companions were trying hard not to display. They'd already spent far too many hours walking for one day, and he knew from experience that being too tired to function often resulted in accidents and mistakes. "I think now would be the best time to have an hour off our feet. We need to stop so we can rest, eat and drink. Stars know how long it'll be 'til we get the chance again."

Jayce made sure not to make eye contact with any of them. The last thing he needed was for Danis or Bastian to think they were responsible for holding them up and try to play the martyr.

"Excellent idea, my darling," Ellie said with a sigh. "I know I'm stuffed, and you guys had already been walking long before I got here. So, what's on the menu? Are you fetching, or should I?"

Jayce laughed, pulling her against him and relishing in the comfort and energy they shared when they touched. Of course, Ellie had heard his worried thoughts in his head and jumped in to avert it from happening. Before he could tell her that they had food and water in the packs he'd supplied, she'd fetched a plate of sandwiches, a plate of honey cakes, six bottles of water and a couple of thermos flasks holding Stars only knew what.

"Do you think this will do for now? I threw it together before I left so I could fetch it if and when we needed it," Ellie said, moving to the grassy area where she'd laid out their meal and sinking to the ground with a moan.

"Fates Ellie, this is amazing," Bastian said, his eyes flicking between the sandwiches and the cakes as if he couldn't decide which to reach for first.

"Yeah, Ellie. I can't even begin to tell you how glad I am you decided to join us," Danis said, not even hesitating before reaching for a honey cake. He moaned after the first bite. "Man… they taste even better than they look."

Without a word, Jayce dropped to the ground before Ellie and began unlacing her boots. He knew she was far from being a weak female who'd complain about walking for four hours while six months pregnant with twins. But if his feet were hurting, which they were, hers would have to be a helleva lot worse.

Ellie looked into his eyes and opened her mouth as

if she wanted to protest against the special treatment. But his look of determination must have changed her mind, because the soft voice in his head saying *thank you, baby* told him everything.

Ellie

ELLIE COULDN'T SUPPRESS the moans of pleasure at the feel of Jayce's hands massaging her aching feet. Knowing what was at stake, she'd have kept going without complaining until she physically couldn't. It was typical of Jayce to insist that they were *all* exhausted and needed to rest. He'd never allow one person to feel they were weak or holding the others back.

"Hey Bastian, can you give us some idea of what to expect once we reach the castle? Like how many doors we might need to get opened before we hit the royal suite?" Ellie asked, trying to shift the attention from her moans.

Bastian and Danis looked at each other and began throwing around ideas about the most direct route to the royal suite. Apparently, the castle was a bit of a maze, and the suite could be reached from several different directions.

Jayce, Bastian and Danis spent the next hour planning and arguing about the ins and outs of reaching the royal suite. But Ellie's attention soon drifted to what she considered other, more important matters. It was the first opportunity she'd had to mull over what she'd learned about the prophecy, especially the part about one of her daughters being the fated mate of a Fae prince. Exactly how that was supposed to work was beyond her wildest imaginings.

Before meeting Bastian and Danis, she'd never really thought about the magical realm that had been shut away for so many years. What would the King of the Spring Court, or any of the other Kings, think of this fated mating? It wasn't like her daughters would have even a drop of Fae blood in their genes. Oh no… only human, dragon and witch blood. In other words, every other race the Fae despised.

Ellie breathed a huge sigh and rubbed her belly. Maybe she should concentrate more on what was happening right now rather than what could happen in eighteen years. As if hearing her thoughts, Ellie felt the babies move until they were nestled under her hands. A surge of frustrated anger flooded her body and soul. Why was this happening? The Stars had better have a damn good reason for allowing this threat against her, Jayce, and their babies.

It'll be okay, mama. Trust in the Stars.

Ellie didn't know whether she wanted to laugh, cry, or scream at the words of the soft voice in her head trying to comfort her. But, as always, the absurdity of the situation won out, and she burst out laughing. She felt, rather than saw, three heads swivel toward where she sat, rolling with laughter, tears running down her face.

Before she could even blink, Jayce was lifting her onto his lap and holding her close. But she couldn't stop. It was as if the floodgates had opened, and all the pent-up emotions poured out, threatening to drown her in their deluge.

Hey, beautiful girl. What's going on? Hearing Jayce's tender words inside her head seemed to calm some of the inner turmoil. He knew from past experience that she'd be unable to speak out loud in this state.

Stars forgive me, Jayce. I was sitting here railing against everything that's been happening, and one of the babies spoke to me. She said it would all be okay and to trust in the Stars. Damnit, Jayce, I'd been in the middle of a rant against the Stars, and then... my unborn child reached out to comfort me. So, I think hysterical laughter was the best of a few possible reactions.

Well, at least we know the Stars haven't abandoned us, even if they chose a rather unconventional way of letting us know.

Ellie felt her hold on reality slowly return in Jayce's warm, loving embrace. Fine, so it would seem that the Stars had a good reason for allowing what was happening to continue. Which meant they had to get to this Oracle and find out what else needed fixing. Because Ellie now knew, without a shadow of a doubt, that the curse had simply been a means to get them to the Oracle. So, if the threat of her losing her babies was just the tip of the iceberg, how much bigger would the rest of the threat be?

CHAPTER TWENTY-TWO

Bastian

Bastian knew without having to be told that Jayce and Ellie were using their telepathic link to communicate. He was relieved to see how easily Jayce could fix whatever had been wrong, but he waited for one of them to speak first. Something told him he shouldn't interrupt their private conversation.

"Sorry, guys," Ellie finally said, lifting her face from where it had been buried in Jayce's shoulder and smiling sheepishly. "I swear I'm not usually the hysterical female type. But between the pregnancy hormones and all this… crap. Well, let's just say everything came to a head, and I lost it."

"Hey, don't you dare apologise," Bastian said with a smile. "With what you've been going through lately, most people would be curled up in the foetal position, unable to speak."

"Yeah," Danis threw in. "What he said!"

Bastian nudged his friend, and they all chuckled, the previous tension melting away. But the entire episode had made one thing very clear in Bastian's mind. They needed to get to the Oracle and do whatever was necessary to get this damn curse removed as soon as possible.

The closer they got to finding the Oracle, the more the words of the old Priestess had started playing over in his mind.

The prophecy warns that the cost of extracting the cure from the Oracle will be higher than you may be prepared to pay. You need to remember what I said when we first met, that the rewards will far outweigh the sacrifices you must make. Because in the end, the choice will be yours and yours alone to make.

What cost would the Oracle demand for the cure to Ellie's curse? He'd discarded the idea that the demand would be for wealth or some form of monetary return. Bastian would never consider that a sacrifice. So, what would it be?

He'd tried to consider what he had that could be taken away from him, but the only things he'd come up with were his life, his magic, or his birthright to inherit the throne. But seriously, what reward could far outweigh his loss of one of those?

"You okay, man?" Danis asked quietly, nudging his arm. "You're looking a bit… sickly. I was gonna say white, but I think it's closer to green."

Bastian pushed all thoughts of possible rewards and sacrifices back into their box. He'd know soon enough, so dwelling on the unknown was a complete waste of his time and effort. He was pretty sure they'd been sitting and resting longer than they'd planned, and it was time to put their recently formulated plans into action.

"All good, my friend. Guess my mind went a bit off track there for a minute," Bastian said, slapping his friend's back and forcing a smile onto his hopefully no longer green face. "Are we good to go?" he asked Jayce and Ellie, watching as Jayce finished tying Ellie's shoelaces.

"Yep," Ellie replied as Jayce helped her to her feet. "Anyone need this leftover food and drinks?" When they all shook their heads, she waved a hand at the food, and Bastian assumed it had gone back to where it came from. "Okay, let's get this over with, shall we?"

Bastian, Danis and Jayce all stood and hoisted their packs onto their backs. Then, walking in silence, they moved toward the entrance to the castle.

Danis

THEIR TREK to the royal suite had been much easier than anticipated. Danis had never really noticed how few doors in the castle were ever closed, apart from those leading to private suites. As they passed the door that he knew led to where his family lived, Danis had to fight the urge to look inside. Who would he find on the other side of that door?

As if he could read the thoughts flitting around in Danis' head, Bastian threw an arm around his friend's shoulder and sighed. "Yeah, man, I get it. But something tells me we're not supposed to know the answers to those questions. It's kind of a relief to already know who we'll find in the royal suite."

Danis nodded, and they moved on. Bastian was right. There was no point dwelling on the unknown, and even less point in looking for answers. Especially since Danis was almost certain those answers would not be what he'd been hoping for.

When they finally reached the royal suite, they hovered nervously outside the door. They hadn't really thought about a plan to get *this* door open. But the last thing any of them had expected was for the door to open in front of them on its own.

Danis stopped just inside the doors of the entrance to the royal suite, stunned by the state of the once-familiar rooms. The entire place seemed to be alive with magic. Shimmering, the walls rippled like water, ghostly visions dancing across their surface—fleeting glimpses of other realms, other times.

A tall, imposing young man stood in the centre of the room, his back to them as he appeared to be studying one of the ever-changing scenes on the wall. There was no way this could be the Oracle. The man looked no older than Jayce. Convinced he must be an assistant or something, Danis scanned the room for another presence, one who more closely resembled the image of the Oracle Danis had formed in his head.

Unable to find anyone else, Danis opened his mouth to ask the man where they could find the Oracle, when the man turned to face them, and Danis' words got stuck in his throat. *Ho-ly Fates!* There was no longer any doubt that this man was the Oracle!

Eyes with the texture and colour of liquid silver shone from his unlined face, appearing to see into their very souls. And although he portrayed an image of youth and vitality, those eyes held a timeless wisdom that spoke of the immeasurable lifetimes they had seen.

The man's voice seemed to resonate within the very walls of the chamber. "I am Orion Myst, although you may know of me as the Oracle, and I've been expecting you." He paused, looking at each of them with those all-knowing eyes. "I promise to explain everything, but first, you all need to come inside. I'm not sure how the guards would react to seeing me standing with my door open and speaking to… well, no one."

The Oracle's words finally broke through Danis'

stupor, and he shook Bastian out of his. "Ummm...
sorry. We, ummm... weren't expecting—"

"No need for apologies, young seer. Please, just
come inside, and we can talk."

Danis gave the man another surprised look. How
had he known Danis was a seer? Then he wanted to
smack himself over the head. The man had known they
were coming. Hell, he'd known they were outside his
door. Of course he knew Danis was a seer.

Danis moved forward into the room, dragging a
still-staring Bastian with him. He was relieved to see
that Jayce and Ellie appeared to have recovered from
their shock, too. Once all four were inside the room,
Orion waved his hand, and the door closed and locked
behind them. At Danis' raised eyebrow, the man merely
shrugged and gave him a knowing smile.

"Were you expecting someone to disturb us?" Danis
asked with the same knowing smile.

"Better to be safe than sorry, I always say." With
that, the Oracle turned and led the way to what Danis
knew had once been the formal dining room. At Bastian's sudden intake of breath, Danis looked around the
once-familiar room, where Bastian had often invited
him to eat with his family. But while the space they
stood in now was like an exact replica of that room, it
was as if it had been deserted and left to rot for years,
maybe even centuries.

"Ah, yes, I'm sorry you had to see this, Sebastian

Evergreen, Prince of the Spring Court. But do not fear. This is merely a representation of what *might* come to pass. As you know, the future is dictated by the choices made and the roads travelled. Now, please sit so we can talk."

The Oracle smiled as he waved a hand over the chairs where he'd indicated they should sit. Instantly, the chairs were restored to their former glory, unlike the previously dilapidated furniture that had looked incapable of bearing the weight of a flea.

As they all moved to sit, the Oracle waved his hand over the section of the table where they'd be seated. The now fully restored polished timber surface was laden with various foods and drinks.

"Why—?" Bastian asked, looking at the restored furniture and then around at the forlorn state of their surroundings.

"Because there's no point, young prince. Why would I waste my time and energy restoring a future I hope never comes to pass?"

Danis' head swivelled toward Jayce at the sound of a low growl emanating from his throat. He sometimes forgot that Jayce was a dragon, but that growl was all the reminder he needed.

"Enough of the riddles and half-explained truths," Jayce said, his tone raw and gruff. "I'm sorry, but with the threat hanging over my family, my patience is at an all-time low. So how about we skip to the part where you tell us the cost of the cure to remove the curse ... please."

The Oracle's brow creased, and he threw Jayce and Ellie a sympathetic smile. "While I would love to concede to your wishes, Jayce Raythawn, Son of the Stars, I'm afraid we have much to discuss before I can answer that question. But know that while you are with me inside this room, the curse will not progress until a resolution has been reached. Does this ease your mind for the moment?"

Danis watched as the tension in Jayce's body seemed to ease at the Oracle's words. He nodded and pulled Ellie's chair closer, wrapping an arm around her waist. A single tear ran down Ellie's beautiful face, and Danis felt his heart clench at her evident relief. Now, he just prayed that Bastian could live with the cost of whatever sacrifice the Oracle demanded.

Ellie

ELLIE HAD PRACTICALLY FALLEN onto the chair as soon as Orion finished restoring it, and what the Oracle had said about the curse not being able to progress any further while they were in the royal suite had been the best news she'd had in ages.

What she hadn't told anyone was that ever since they'd entered the castle, her headaches had been replaced by a bone-weary exhaustion she'd never have thought possible. It was like the curse had intensified to a level where she was being affected the same as her babies.

She knew she needed to focus on whatever the Oracle was about to tell them, but she had to use all her remaining energy just to stay upright in her chair. Okay, so maybe her symptoms couldn't get any worse while inside the royal suite, but she'd already been struggling to stay conscious before they'd arrived.

Then Orion's melodic voice filled the chamber, each word resonating with an otherworldly power, and she managed to concentrate on the sound. "Sebastian Evergreen. To prove you are worthy of claiming the cure for the Withering Curse, you must first undergo three trials. These trials will be intense and are not for the faint of heart, young prince. You must traverse the Shadowlands, face the Echoes of Regret, and ultimately confront the Void itself."

Orion's grave words sent a chill down Ellie's spine, and her hand instinctively moved to cover her belly. Even the shimmering walls of the chamber seemed to darken, the ever-changing scenes becoming more oppressive.

Bastian's skin had turned a ghastly shade of white, but he nodded resolutely. "I understand," he said, his voice barely above a whisper. "So can we just get on with it… please." Ellie almost smiled at the way Bastian had tacked on a *please* at the end, just as Jayce had.

CHAPTER TWENTY-THREE

Orion Myst (The Oracle)

"Orion Myst," the dragon shifter said in a voice radiating tension, pulling everyone's attention to him. "Can you help us or not?"

Orion sighed and nodded. "Indeed, I can. But the help you shall receive may not be in the form of the help you expect."

Orion could feel the frustration, fear, hope, and so many other emotions emanating from the four people around him. He empathised with their situation, but he could only do and say what he was allowed to.

"The first thing you need to understand is exactly where you are," Orion said, raising his hand to silence the questions he knew were coming. "This entire suite exists at the junction of all possible futures. The visions you see," he gestured to the shimmering walls, "are fragments of what *may* come to pass."

Bastian's eyes flicked between the images, his eyes wide with wonder. "It's incredible," he breathed.

Orion nodded. "Incredible, yes. But also terrible. For with knowledge comes great responsibility and the burden of making seemingly impossible choices."

Orion looked around at the four young faces glued to his as he prepared to tell them what they needed to know. He couldn't remember ever being that young; he wasn't sure he had been. His memories spanned many centuries yet seemed to always portray him as the same young man he appeared to be today. He'd been dreading this day for so long that he couldn't remember when he hadn't known what he now knew. Still… it was time. He cleared his throat and began to speak.

"Jayce Raythawn," he began, fixing his eyes on the dragon shifter's face. "Leader of the Dragon Council, torn between duty and love. Your greatest fear is failing those who depend on you." Jayce's jaw clenched as if to confirm what Orion had said, a muscle twitching in his cheek.

"Sebastian Evergreen," Orion continued. "Heir to the throne of the Spring Court. Haunted by your desire for acceptance. You fear the choices you must make and the destiny you must fulfil." Bastian's eyes widened as a flicker of unease crossed his face.

"And Danis Farsight," the Oracle said with a sigh,

trying to hide his empathy for this young man who had chosen to stand by his friend despite having nothing to gain. "You are the seer of hidden truths, yet you fear the very power that defines you." Danis just nodded, as if the Oracle's words were nothing he hadn't already known.

Finally, Orion's attention settled on Ellie. Despite her weakened state and debilitating fear for her unborn babies, she met his gaze with an unflinching stare. He had to suppress his smile as she spoke before he could. Of course, this one would need to have her say first.

"Orion," Ellie said, her voice low but firm. "I need to know the truth. My babies—" She paused, looking down at her belly as if to draw his attention to the subjects of her question. "Can the curse that threatens them be broken?"

"Ellie Raythawn," he said softly, compassion and respect for this brave woman conjuring memories of friends and lovers long forgotten. "Half-mortal, half-witch. Your journey has already been one of many trials, yet your greatest challenge lies ahead."

"Fine. Then just tell me what I have to do already," she insisted. "Stars, I don't care what it is; I'd do anything to keep my family safe."

Orion nodded slowly. "As you have proven on many occasions. Your protective instincts serve you well, Daughter of the Stars. But remember, sometimes the greatest act of protection is to let go."

"What's that supposed to mean?" she demanded,

fear and determination warring within her eyes. "What do I need to let go of?"

Orion heaved a sigh and rubbed his forehead. He'd forgotten how gruelling the task of delivering bad news could be. But he knew it was time for them to hear the truth.

"This world in which you stand," he began, his words measured and heavy with significance, "is the current future of the realms. A future where your twin baby girls..." He paused, wishing he didn't have to be the bearer of such tragic news. "I'm sorry, but they did not survive the curse."

Orion watched the blood drain from Ellie's stricken face. "Wait... that's ridiculous," she whispered. "How could that even be possible? Jayce, tell him he's wrong," she cried in a broken voice as Jayce's arm tightened around her.

Jayce was as pale as his wife, but he spoke to Orion in a calm, steady voice. "I think you need to explain what's going on."

Orion sighed, already feeling worn out by the emotional turmoil surrounding him. How could he explain the complexities of what most people regarded simply as fate? "While you appear to be standing inside one of the many potential futures of the realms, you are, in reality, merely standing on the outside looking in. In your reality, as it now exists, your babies are still safely growing inside their mother's womb. I cannot even begin to explain how this situation is possible, but it is, and it is not within our power to question such things."

"Okay, so I guess I'll just have to take your word for all that," Ellie said, her voice stronger now. "So, do we even know what to do to prevent this future from happening? Or is that just another thing we don't have the power to question?"

Orion bit back the smile the young morwitch's sassy words almost provoked. She had every right to be pissed at the situation she was in. She'd done everything right in her past, and now her future happiness was being ripped out from under her.

"Look, I already knew I would be the one responsible for the price of the cure. What I still don't know is what that price will be," Bastian said, and Orion was impressed by the set of the boy's chin.

"What do you know of the fated mate bond?" Orion interrupted, his voice cutting through the tension like a knife. "It is both a blessing and a curse, is it not, young prince of the Fae?"

Bastian's pale silver eyes were clouded with confusion. "Wait, I didn't choose any of this," he said softly. "I know next to nothing about how the mate bond works, but I would never deny its existence. This bond between myself and one of Ellie's babies... it is in the far distant future. So, are you saying it's somehow connected to saving the twins' lives?"

"Wait, I'm sure I already read this book," Ellie said, her sarcasm barely veiled. "This is the future unless something we do prevents it from happening?" The Oracle seemed to be studying Ellie like a bug under a microscope. "Yeah, this is not the first Prophecy we've had to deal with," she said, grabbing Jayce's hand and squeezing it.

"I understand that you know how prophecies usually work, but this particular prophecy is like no other in the history of the worlds. You see, the Stars and the Fates created this prophecy as a reward in response to the prayers of millions. In fact, it's more like a second chance than a prophecy. A chance to right the wrongs that resulted in this future you now see."

Not surprised by the looks of shock and confusion on the faces around him, Orion sighed in resignation. Those looks would soon be replaced by ones of shock, horror, and dread.

"I think it's best to begin at the time and place you were in before coming to Brevis. Ellie, as you know, a curse was placed on you that, if left to run its course, would result in the death of your babies in utero. In this future we now inhabit, that curse succeeded."

Ellie's sob, Jayce's growl, and the whitish/green shade of Danis and Bastian's faces were exactly as he'd anticipated. Orion merely held up his hand, and the group again grew silent. "You need to remember that none of the options or foreknowledge you now have existed at that time. Ellie blamed herself for the babies' death and sank into a deep depression. So, when rumours that the twins had died as a result of a curse placed on Ellie by a Fae, Jayce had flown into a rage the likes of which no one had ever seen."

"Of course I did. What else would you expect from a grieving father?" Jayce growled.

"I *understand* the actions of everyone involved. I don't wish to sound indifferent or unemotional, but you must remember that I am merely relating past events. What I am telling you is not my opinion about those events, just the facts. Hopefully, that error will soon be rectified and the future rewritten accordingly. So... are we all ready for me to continue?" Orion looked around the table to see four heads nodding and picked up from where he'd left off.

"Unfortunately, the fallout from the babies' deaths was so much more far-reaching than could ever have been anticipated. When it became known that the Fae Realm had been using the mortal realm as a dumping ground for their banished criminals, the realms descended into chaos."

"The Dragon and Witch Realms allied and declared war on the Fae. Thus began many years of bloodshed and hatred among the races. Unable to breach the wards around the Fae realm, they focused on eliminating every Fae they could find in the Mortal Realm."

"Now, it is time to view how these events affected those in the Fae Realm. Unaware of the banished Valerian's misdeeds, the four kings of the Fae Realms continued to rule in blissful ignorance for a time. When news of what was happening outside their realm seeped in, dissension among the four Kings quickly grew out of control. The courts were divided over how best to deal with the situation, resulting in assassination attempts on those in power. I'm sorry young prince, but your father was the first to fall. Voicing his beliefs that reopening the wards and arranging talks with the leaders of the other realms ended up signing his own death warrant."

"The assassination of the King of the Spring Court sparked what became known as the War of the Kings. The realm became divided, and basically, civil war broke out. They denied the Dragon and Witch realms the pleasure of destroying them and did it themselves from within. By the time I was sent by the Fates to restore order to the realm, none of the Kings had survived. You, young prince, renounced your claim to the throne, too broken by the deaths of all those you loved and the travesty that had befallen all of the Fae Realm.

"So… now that you know how we came to be in this version of the future, it's time to discuss the cost of changing it for the better. I'm sure you have been told that acquiring a boon from the Oracle comes at a great price. And although you will all be affected by the outcome, it is Prince Sebastian who must agree to pay that price."

CHAPTER TWENTY-FOUR

Ellie

Jayce opened his mouth to speak, whether to offer to take Bastian's place or demand more answers, Ellie would never know. A searing pain ripped through her abdomen driving a scream from her throat. What in all the realms was happening? It felt like someone, or something was trying to pull the babies out through her stomach.

"Ellie!" Jayce cried, reaching out to catch her just before she toppled out of her chair. Her head was spinning, and the connection with her babies seemed to flicker like a weak lightbulb about to go out.

"The babies," she breathed, her hands clenching tightly around Jayce's shirt, desperation flooding her voice. "Something's wrong. It feels like… Oh, Stars, Jayce, I think I'm losing them."

She felt the panic erupt around her, the frantic voices in the chamber blending into a chaotic maelstrom of concern and fear, but all she could focus on was the growing sense of dread in her heart and the look on Jayce's face ravaged by fear as he leaned over her.

"What the hell, Orion?" Jayce snarled. "You said the curse couldn't progress while we were with you?"

"I'm sorry, Jayce. This shouldn't be possible. I have no idea how—"

"Stay with me, beautiful girl," Jayce pleaded, his voice cracking. "You just need to hold on. Don't let go."

Wait... let go? Wasn't that what the Oracle had said she needed to do? Was this what he'd been talking about?

Ellie tried to respond, but the words wouldn't come. Instead, her mind was flooded with images of how the future should have been.

She and Jayce sitting in bed, each with a baby girl cradled in their arms.

Two little girls squealing in delight as their Daddy chases them around the yard.

The visions continued, each showing her beautiful babies as they grew. It could have been so wonderful…

She could feel herself slipping away, fighting to hold onto the connection to her babies as it grew fainter with each passing second. Darkness began to intrude on the edges of her vision as she slowly lost her hold on the world. With her last conscious thought, she sent out a desperate prayer to whatever entity may have been listening:

Please, let our babies live.

Jayce

A STUNNED SILENCE filled the room, all eyes on Ellie as they waited to see if her chest would continue to rise and fall. Jayce cradled her in his arms, his eyes wild with fear as he looked up at the others.

"She's still alive, and so are the babies. I can feel them through our bond. But we need to do something, *now*!" he demanded, his voice raw with emotion. "Orion, how do we save them?"

"I need to begin the trials," Bastian announced, stepping forward to stand beside the Oracle. "Isn't that the only way to save Ellie and the twins and thus change the future?"

All eyes turned to Orion. Jayce closed his eyes, praying that his wife and babies would live. He knew without a shadow of a doubt that his own life would be over if he lost them. Anger at how the Fates had screwed them over seeped into his veins. After they'd done everything the Stars had asked of them, this was how they were repaid?

Clenching his jaw, Jayce gently lowered Ellie to the floor. Then he shot to his feet, the weight of his own frustration and feelings of inadequacy threatening to pull him under. This entire situation was beyond ridiculous. "Okay, I've had more than enough of this prophecy crap. This is all wrong. *I* need to be the one to face the trials. These are *my* family's lives at stake. There's no way I'm going to sit back and let someone else do my job," he growled, his entire body wracked with guilt over what he considered his failure to protect his family. "What good am I if I can't even protect those I love?"

Bastian's gaze flickered to Ellie's pale face, then to the desperation Jayce knew was in his eyes. "Come on, Jayce. You *are* protecting those you love. They need you here, and they need you to stay safe."

Jayce's hand moved to his chest, where the faint thrumming of his connection to Ellie pulsed weakly. The thought of her fading life force only made everything feel more complicated. "Bastion, I can't let you risk everything," he finally said, his voice ragged with emotion, "while I just... sit here watching and waiting."

He watched as Bastian straightened, determination radiating from every pore. "It's okay, Jayce. My gut is telling me that we're both doing exactly what we're supposed to do. And I always trust my gut."

Jayce's respect and admiration for the young Fae

prince warred with his conflicted emotions, making Jayce feel like a deflated balloon. He knew Bastian was right, that Ellie and the babies needed him to be there, but the guilt still hung heavy in his chest. "Fine. I may not be able to do this myself," Jayce said, "but I swear I'll try to find a way to help. Somehow."

A moan from the other side of the room drew everyone's attention. Danis sat slumped with his head in his visibly shaking hands. He was murmuring incoherently and appeared to be panting as if he'd just run a marathon.

"Danis? What's going on, man?" Jayce called, his worry increasing yet again.

Danis lifted his head from his hands, his eyes struggling to focus on the group. "Oh, by the Fates, I saw… I saw…" he moaned again, shaking his head like a dog shaking off water.

Bastian was kneeling in front of Danis in an instant, squeezing his friend's shoulders as if trying to bring his focus to him. "It's okay, Dan. We just need you to tell us what you saw, okay?" he asked, his voice warm and reassuring.

Danis sucked in a shaky breath, his eyes finally meeting Bastian's. "Fates, Bastian. I saw… I guess they were possible futures. So many futures, all tangled together like threads in a tapestry." His voice grew steadier as he continued to speak. "In one, I saw the twins, all grown up and as beautiful as their mother." He looked to Jayce with an attempt at a smile. But it was quickly replaced by fear and dread as he again gazed at nothing. "In another one, there was nothing but darkness... everywhere."

He shuddered and again dipped his head to the floor. "Then there were the others..." He trailed off, his pain-filled eyes lifting to look into Bastian's.

"What about the others, Dan? You need to tell us *everything* you saw." Bastian asked softly.

"Well, in some of the visions, you succeeded. In the trials, I mean," Danis spoke slowly. "But in some of the others... well, you didn't do so good."

Jayce sucked in a breath and drew Ellie closer, his jaw locked tight. Bastian had turned that pale green colour again.

Orion's melodic voice pierced the tension. "The future is not set, my young prince. These visions are but possibilities, determined by the choices you've yet to make."

Danis

DANIS WATCHED the effect of his words on his friends and wished he'd never had the damn visions. Attempting to restore his equilibrium and push away the visions he wished he could unsee, Danis turned to the Oracle. One of the visions he'd glimpsed had raised some questions. "So, do the rules say I can't go into the trials with Bastian?"

He watched the expressions on the Oracle's face change from surprise to speculation. Determined to ignore the protests from those around him, Danis saw the moment the Oracle's expression changed to understanding. Danis had no intention of telling anyone the details of his visions, but from the look Orion was now giving him, Danis assumed the man had guessed what was behind his question.

The visions had been a jumbled mess of possible outcomes. But one had stood out from the others as if Danis was meant to see it. Bastian had obviously been inside one of the trials, but somehow, Danis had been standing beside him.

"Hmmm... interesting question, young seer. While the prophecy states that Sebastian must be the one to complete the trials, I cannot recall the word "alone" or any such connotation of the word being included."

"And can we watch Bastian's progression through the trials?"

"Of course, if that is what you wish," Orion replied with a raised eyebrow.

"Yep, I do," Danis said, relieved and terrified at the same time. He had no idea which of the three trials showed Danis helping his friend. All Danis knew was that in the one where he helped, Bastian emerged from the trial victorious.

Well, at least he knew which trial Bastian would need his help with. The image of the two altars was burned into his brain. Now, he just had to placate his friends' concerns and wait until he was needed.

Damnit... he'd always hated that *wait* word.

CHAPTER TWENTY-FIVE

Bastian

Bastian wanted nothing more than to run screaming from the place as the enormity of what he'd committed to doing settled on his shoulders. But he knew that nothing he said or did now would change anything. "It doesn't matter what Danis saw. We already knew that the possible outcomes were limitless. It also doesn't matter what challenges the trials present. I need to face them."

Bastian felt a blend of courage and resignation wash over him just from saying the words out loud. He thought of his people in the Spring Court, of the expectations placed upon him since birth. But more than that, he thought of the agonised looks on his new friends' faces when they considered the possibility of failure.

"Bastian, you don't have to—" Jayce began, but Bastian shook his head.

"Yes, Jayce, you and I both know that I do," Bastian interrupted. "I'll do whatever it takes to save Ellie and your babies.

Or die trying, he added silently.

BASTIAN STOOD at the entrance to the trial chamber, his heart pounding in his chest. Energy and magic pulsed through the air in front of him, and he clenched his fists. It was time…

"Are you prepared, young prince?" Orion's voice floated over into the shadowy room.

Bastian tried to swallow, but his mouth was too dry. "Ready as I'll ever be," he replied, mortified by the tremor in his voice.

"Remember, the trials will test more than just your strength. They will challenge your very sense of self."

Nodding grimly, Bastian sucked in a deep breath and looked into the chamber before him. He sighed in relief at the sight of the familiar lush, vibrant world of the Spring Court stretching off into the distance. At least he'd know where he was going.

As soon as he stepped forward and crossed the chamber's threshold, he realised it had all been an illusion, merely portraying what his mind had wanted to see. The vision of the Spring Court melted away as the world around him blurred and shifted. When his vision cleared, he thought his legs might give way beneath him.

The Spring Court was gone. In its place stood a frozen wasteland blanketed in snow. Icy winds howled, carrying mournful, unintelligible cries that seemed to come from every direction.

"Oh please, by the Fates, no," Bastian whispered in horror. "This could never really happen. It has to be an illusion."

Stumbling forward, Bastian tried to ignore the bone-numbing cold penetrating his clothing. Every inhale was sheer torment, as though the icy air was searing his lungs. The entire land was caught in winter's cruel grip. But the saddest part—everything about this place felt so real.

Stop it! It's all an illusion. Bastian had to keep reminding himself, as fear and doubt tried to erase all hope of succeeding.

Just. Stay. Focused.

But as he pressed on through the desolate landscape, the anguished voices grew louder, filling the air around him as the words became recognisable. They were screaming accusations.

You failed us, Prince Sebastian.

How could you let this happen?

We loved and trusted you.

Bastian squeezed his eyes shut, wishing it were that easy to block out the sounds. Okay, he needed to pull himself together. He knew he hadn't failed anyone. In fact, if he could push past the horrifying illusions and achieve his goal of surviving the trials, no one would ever be able to accuse him of failing in his duties. And this world surrounding him would cease to exist.

When he opened his eyes again, he felt his earlier determination rise to the surface. "I will *not* fail," he yelled into the icy wind. "None of this is real. And no matter what it takes, I will *never* allow this to become a reality."

Bastian trudged forward, continuing his battle against the relentless snow, his boots crunching over the ice beneath them. As he rounded a frost-covered hill, his breath caught in his throat.

An endless field of ice sculptures lay before him—men, women and children frozen in twisted poses of agony. Their faces were contorted in silent screams, eyes pleading for help that never came. *This* was where the voices were coming from.

"Not. Real." Bastian muttered, his voice shaking. But his resolve began to crumble when he started to recognise familiar faces, some he'd known since he was a small child. Their eyes seemed to bore into him, filled with disappointment, disgust, and despair.

"None of this is my fault. Stop blaming me..." he cried, unaware that his mind was beginning to acknowledge the illusions as if they were real.

"Bastian..." the voice calling his name was so faint that Bastian wondered if he'd imagined it. Heart pounding, he spun in the direction he thought the voice had come from.

Ellie... She sat at the edge of the frozen field, a small, wrapped bundle in each arm. The image of the three—a broken, withered woman holding what Bastian knew were the lifeless bodies of the twins—flickered like a candle in the wind, growing more transparent with each passing moment.

"Ellie!" Bastian rushed toward where she stood. But every time he thought he was getting closer, she remained just out of reach.

"Bastian... Why didn't you save us?" Ellie's voice was fading along with her ghostly image. "You were supposed to save us...

Bastian fell to his knees, desperation and fear tearing through him. "I'm trying," he choked out. "I swear, I'm doing everything I can." Again, he'd acknowledged the illusion.

As the ghostly forms faded away to nothing, doubt crashed over Bastian like a tidal wave. How could he hope to save an entire realm when he couldn't even protect those closest to him? "Damnit, what if they're right, and I'm just not strong enough." Bastian's voice was harsh and broken. "What if I need help?"

As if in answer to his question, an image of two beautiful woman who bore a strong resemblance to Ellie flashed into his mind. They appeared to be in their late teens and stood laughing and talking together. Bastian's breath caught as the two paused in their laughter and seemed to be looking directly at him. Their eyes were a perfect blend of their parents, Ellie and Jayce, the greenish-gold sparkling with mischief. They both smiled and nodded at him, then returned to their conversation.

As the image faded, Bastian felt his determination return, his body suffused with hope for the possible future he had glimpsed. That was the true future, not the horror-filled illusions surrounding him that filled his mind with despair.

Bastian pushed himself to his feet, fists clenched at his sides. "No," he growled into the bitter wind that sought to destroy him. "I will make *that* future a reality… for all of us. Damn it all to the depths of hell. There must be a way to ensure Ellie's babies will survive to grow into those beautiful young women. And I intend to find it."

Bastian's mind clung to the images of the two happy and healthy women and the possible future they represented as he pushed on through the frozen nightmare. Pushing away the despair still trying to claw its way to the surface, he held tight to the ember of hope burning in his chest.

Without warning, the icy landscape around him began to shimmer and warp. The frozen wasteland seemed to dissolve, and Bastian stumbled in shock as he recognised the familiar surroundings taking shape around him. He was in his bedroom in the Fae Castle, well, more like the bedroom he'd had as a child, complete with cherished mementoes and toys he hadn't seen in years.

"To progress, you must sacrifice. Choose wisely, young Prince Sebastian. You may keep only one." The disembodied voice echoed through the air as if coming from everywhere and nowhere at the same time.

"What the…?" Bastian began to ask but knew it was pointless. The voice had spoken, and he needed to figure out the rest on his own.

Bastian's heart clenched as he realised what the trial demanded. His gaze fell upon three objects, each pulsing with magical energy: a wooden figurine his father had carved for him when he was five years old, a sword Danis had given him for his thirteenth birthday, and a portrait of his parents, the King and Queen of the Spring Court, on their thrones.

"No," Bastian whispered, his voice cracking. "Please, don't make me choose."

But the voice remained silent, leaving him to grapple with the impossible decision. He knew what he was being asked to do. Each of the three objects represented a piece of the future Bastian had hoped to achieve. To win his father's love and approval, to become a brave and proficient fighter, and to sit on the throne as King of the Spring Court.

But surely he needed to attain the first two before he could claim the third? How the Fates was he supposed to choose just one? Wait… what if he chose the wrong one? Was there even a clear right and wrong choice?

Bastian slumped to the floor, a tear sliding down his cheek as he stared at the three objects—all of his life goals needing to be narrowed down to one choice. The room shifted, growing colder.

And that's when he knew the answer. He needed to choose the throne. How else could he prevent the horrific futures he'd witnessed since this all began? What kind of leader puts his own desires before those of his people? The first two objects represented his personal desires. The third was his destiny.

Bastian got to his feet and declared his choice in a loud, clear voice. "I choose the third object. I choose to be King!"

Suddenly, the room darkened, and a figure materialised before him—an older version of himself, eyes hollow with despair and defeat.

"What makes you think you have what it takes to be a king? I am your future," the shade intoned, its voice a haunting echo of Bastian's own. "You'll fail them all. Your people will suffer, the babies will die, and you will never have a fated mate."

Bastian recoiled, shaking his head violently. "I don't believe you. You may embody the person I would have become before these trials, but you're too late. I know who I am now, and what I need to do. There's no way I'll ever let you exist!"

The shade laughed, his face and voice filled with derision. "You're not strong enough. You never were. Just give up now and spare yourself the pain."

For a moment, Bastian wavered, the crushing weight of his responsibilities threatening to overwhelm him. But then, he thought of everything he'd achieved already, and a new spark of defiance ignited.

"Okay, maybe you're partly right," Bastian said, pinning the shade in place with an angry stare. "I may not be strong enough alone. But I don't have to be." He thought of his new friends, Ellie and Jayce, who already felt more like family than his real one. Even though they'd only known each other for such a short time, something about working together towards a worthy goal made time irrelevant.

Then he thought of his best friend, Danis. He'd been under no obligation to travel to Brevis and help them. Yet he'd chosen to stay by Bastian's side, just like the brother Bastian had always considered him to be. "I have the love and support of friends who've become like family. And together, we'll destroy this horror-filled future and restore the realms to their former glory."

The shade began to flicker, doubt creeping into its hollow eyes. Bastian took advantage of its wavering retreat and stepped forward, his voice loud, and clear, and strong.

"You lose, shade. I choose love," he declared. "I

choose to keep fighting. And I choose hope, no matter what it costs."

As Bastian's words echoed through the chamber, the illusion around him began to crumble, the strength of his character demolishing the last vestige of the nightmarish trial.

Stumbling out of the illusion, Bastian gasped for breath. He felt like he'd been trapped underwater and had finally reached the surface. His legs trembled, threatening to give way beneath him. He braced himself against the cold stone wall of the Fae Castle as he fought to regain control of his emotions.

"I did it," he said in a harsh whisper. "I can't believe I actually did it."

Bastian knew this was only the beginning. But the weight of responsibility he'd been carrying since this all began seemed to have lessened thanks to his success in the first trial. Maybe he *could* do this.

Well, one down, two to go. Sucking in a deep breath, he pushed away from the wall. He was ready to face the next challenge with eyes wide open… wasn't he?

CHAPTER TWENTY-SIX

Jayce

J ayce let out the breath he hadn't realised he'd been holding as he watched Bastian exit the first trial a winner. He was torn between his pride in Bastian's accomplishment and his envy at not being involved.

See, he is fine doing it without your help, his annoying inner voice taunted.

Yeah, well, I never said he wouldn't be.

True... but you definitely thought it.

Oh, shut up.

Jayce's eyes never left Bastian's form as the fae prince slumped down against the wall and caught his breath. No matter what anyone said, Jayce couldn't shake the weight of his own inadequacy pressing down on him once again.

He wondered what had prompted Danis to ask Orion whether anyone was allowed to help Bastian complete the trials. It had been just after the visions of the future, so the question had to be related to something he'd seen.

But Jayce knew without asking that the others wouldn't let him into the trials to help Bastian. The problem had never been about Jayce's ability to conquer the trials. It was about Ellie and the babies not being left alone, and some of his frustration faded once he'd accepted that truth.

Without conscious thought, Jayce rubbed the spot on his chest where Ellie's life force continued to pulse weakly. The thought of losing her had him almost paralysed with fear.

"I know I need to be here for you and the babies, sweetheart, but being forced to just watch and wait, knowing Bastian is risking everything, is killing me," Jayce whispered, wishing he could at least talk to Elle so they could share the waiting.

He watched as Bastian straightened, determination again radiating from the young prince. Jayce felt a surge of admiration mingled with his conflicted emotions. He wanted to call out, to offer encouragement, but the rules of the trials forbade it.

"You've got this, Bastian," he said softly, knowing his words wouldn't reach the prince. "Please make it through this. For Ellie's sake... hell, for all our sakes."

Jayce watched as Bastian took a deep breath,

squaring his shoulders for the next challenge. The dragon shifter's hands clenched into fists, his own resolve strengthening alongside Bastian's. His gaze darted between the still form of Ellie on the bed and the shimmering barrier that separated him from Bastian's trials.

"Jayce?" Ellie's voice was little more than a whisper.

Jayce was beside her in a heartbeat, his hand reaching for hers as he threaded their fingers together. "Hey, beautiful girl. Welcome back," he crooned.

Her fingers squeezed his. "Jayce. Where's Bastian... is he...?"

Jayce swallowed back a groan. Of course, that would be the first thing she asked him. Torn between honesty and wanting to comfort Ellie, he chose to tell her the truth. "Bastian has already started the trials. He's beaten the first one and is about to return for the second. The boy is doing a damn fine job so far. I might even be warming up to the idea of him being our son-in-law."

Fear flashed in Ellie's beautiful eyes. "Wait... he went in alone? Oh, baby, you should be with him. He needs you."

"No," Jayce said firmly, even as doubt gnawed at him. "Bastian is doing us all proud. I need to be here with you and the babies."

Ellie's eyes met his, understanding and love soothing his sore heart. "Okay... those are the last words I ever expected to hear from your mouth. So, you are actually handling stepping back and letting Bastian do this without you?"

"Well, it hasn't been easy. But I'm managing," Jayce knew he was blushing, but he'd decided Ellie didn't need the extra stress of hearing about how much he'd struggled with his responsibilities.

"Right… so I pass out for like five minutes, and you decide to act like a mature adult for a change. Unbelievable!"

Damn, it was good to have his Ellie back.

Danis

WATCHING his best friend struggle with the harsh life choices of the first trial was one of the hardest things Danis had ever done. Growing up as close as brothers, he and Bastian had always tackled their problems together. Yet here Danis was, standing back and watching the entire ordeal like a useless spectator.

It was killing him not being able to help. The Oracle had erected a transparent magical barrier between where they sat watching and the Trial Chamber. Which meant Danis couldn't even shout his congratulations and encouragement to Bastian as he emerged victorious from the first trial.

Well, at least Danis knew he hadn't been needed in the first trial. He'd memorised the details of the scenario in which Bastian would need his help, warning Orion that he *might* need the shield dropped at a moment's notice. Okay, so Danis knew that the word *might* didn't really apply, but he hadn't wanted to give too much away or have to answer any questions.

He watched Bastian step away from the wall he'd been leaning on, preparing to face the second trial. Danis wished for the umpteenth time that there was something—hell, anything—he could do to help his friend succeed. But knowing he'd be able to help Bastian when his friend most needed it would have to do. For now, Danis just had to pray that the path they were currently on was the one toward the future in which he helped Bastian emerge victorious. He refused to even consider any of the other possible outcomes he'd seen.

CHAPTER TWENTY-SEVEN

Bastian

After pushing away from the wall, Bastian took a few tentative steps forward. His head and muscles ached, a consequence of the mental and emotional toll the first trial had taken. But he'd made it through the first task. Now, he needed to prove it wasn't just a fluke. Ellie and the twins were counting on him.

Knowing that whatever he saw from outside the entrance to the second trial would be an illusion, Bastian crossed the threshold and stood perfectly still. Just as it had in the first trial, the air around him began to shimmer as the landscape rearranged itself into whatever horror he would face next. About to take a step forward onto what appeared to be a solid stone floor, Bastian's eyes widened as the floor suddenly began to ripple like water.

"What the—" was all he managed to get out before the world around him erupted into a chaotic nightmare. Where there'd previously been walls, jagged rock formations now jutted out at impossible angles, surrounded by patches of ground that swirled and shifted like quicksand. Bastian felt as if his heart would leap out of his chest as he surveyed the impossibly treacherous terrain that seemed to defy logic itself.

"O-kay," he breathed, reminding himself over and over that this all had to be an illusion. "Everything is just fine. Nothing here is real, so it can't hurt me… right?"

He gulped when he caught sight of what looked like hundreds of thorny vines just beyond the rock formations. They appeared to be alive, slithering over the rocks like snakes. Something glinted in the shadowed light, and Bastian was pretty sure it was the sharp, prickly barbs that coated the vines.

He jumped as a loud rumbling sound permeated the air, followed by the ominous sight of the ground in front of him splitting and crumbling away to form a large chasm. If Bastian had been one step closer, he'd have been a lot more than six feet under by now.

"Not. Fine!" Bastian cried, backing away from the newly formed pit of doom. "Nothing about any of this will ever be fine!

He scanned the ever-changing landscape, searching

for any sign of a safe path forward. Time was of the essence, but one wrong move could spell disaster.

He closed his eyes and tried to focus on the problem, praying that a solution would come to him. He was a fae of the Spring Court. His magic could manipulate plant life, as well as air and water. There had to be a way through this. He just needed to think!

As ideas for how he could use his magic to help him navigate his way past the current problem emerged, Bastian squared his shoulders and felt his hope rekindle. "Okay, then," he said, his voice growing stronger. "Time to just suck it up and get this over with." So many people were counting on him to make it through these trials.

Fine, he'd just go around the damn crater and figure it out as he went.

But as soon as he began to step cautiously around the edge of the Fates-be-damned chasm, he knew he'd made a mistake. Exactly *why* he'd expected it to be as easy as just going around the monstrosity proved just how gullible he was. Like *anything* in these damned trials would be that easy. So, he wasn't all that surprised when the solid ground he'd just been walking on suddenly turned into quicksand.

His left foot sank into the ground as if it had been swallowed whole, while his right remained on the only section of solid ground still intact. Panic surged through him. What in all the realms was he supposed to do now?

"Unbelievable! You do realise how totally ridiculous this all is, right?" Bastian shouted, his voice directed toward the sky. Surely *some* god-like entity could hear him? This was utter bullshit, and the trial had only just begun.

With his left leg sinking further into the quicksand with each passing second, maintaining his balance was quickly becoming almost impossible. Trying to think while wobbling unsteadily, he felt something warm and ball-shaped appear in his hand. He could feel it pulsing softly even before he saw it. *Now what?*

Use your magic, you idiot! Bastian called on his magic and directed it toward the treacherous earth. He sighed in relief when small roots and vines emerged from the still-hard earth and crept toward where he stood. Gripping whatever greenery he could reach, he pulled himself free with a resounding squelch.

"Well, at least something finally worked the way it was supposed to," he panted, falling to his knees, wiping the sweat from his face and sucking in huge gulps of air. Which was when the small roots and simple vines began to morph into the thorny vines he'd seen earlier. *Of course he'd spoken too soon!*

As more of the vicious appendages erupted from the ground, they began to writhe and strike out like feral snakes. Bastian's eyes widened as he was forced to duck and weave to avoid their reach. "Oh, come on!" he shouted as the deadly thorns raked across the skin on his arm. He looked down and remembered the orb in his hand. Had the thorns been trying to get to it?

Clutching it tighter, he knew that whatever the orb held, it was way too important to risk losing. Then, desperate to escape the vines and find out what the orb contained, he summoned a gust of wind and wrapped himself inside it, the wind lifting him over the unstable ground and pushing back the vines. After clearing a path through them until he was out of their reach, he lifted his hand holding the orb and stared at the pulsing energy encased within. Wait… was that two separate pulses of energy? *Holy Fates preserve us. The orb contained the energy of the unborn twins.*

Bastian released the wind from around him and took in his new surroundings. They hadn't really changed much, but at least the ground felt a bit firmer where he'd landed. "It's okay, little ones. I'll get us out of here… somehow," he promised, the old determination surging through him stronger than before. It was as if carrying the orb made everything feel more real.

As if responding to what it perceived as a taunt, the ground once again fell away in front of him, and he immediately recalled the wind. Then he alternated between running and using the wind to leap over the seemingly never-ending chasms. Stumbling a couple of times on his landing, he quickly regained his footing and pushed on for what felt like hours. Bastian's muscles screamed, and his lungs burned as he continued through what had begun to feel like a minefield. He clutched the orb firmly against his chest, its faint pulse no match for the frantic beating of his own heart.

Bastian finally slowed when he realised the chasms had become fewer and farther apart. His legs screamed for this to be the break he'd been praying for. Slowing to a walk, he sucked huge gulps of air into his burning lungs.

As if on cue, flames erupted around him, caging him in, the heat searing his skin. Wait… had he really just *thought* the word burning, and this had happened? He suddenly had an overwhelming urge to just scream and tell whoever was listening what they could do with their stupid trial. He was even beginning to wonder which would break first... his mind or his body.

Then, as if to remind him why he was even inside this deathtrap, he felt the orb pulse a little faster in his hand. Shit… the babies… Ellie. What the hell was he thinking just standing inside the walls of fire inching closer with every second.

Pulling himself together, Bastian called on water and created a shield of ice around himself, the opposing magic hissing as the flames tried to reach him. Feeling the ice thinning from the constant onslaught, he inched forward step by agonising step, holding his breath and praying the ice held long enough as he plunged through the fiery walls.

Come on, man. You can do this...

Sweating as if he'd run a marathon, Bastian

emerged from the flames and released the thin layer of ice still surrounding him. Checking that the orb in his hand still pulsed, he pushed his weary limbs forward.

It wasn't long before the air once again began to shimmer, and a towering maze of mirrors replaced the previous landscape. Bastian's reflection stared back at him, looking far more confident than he felt.

"Riigghhtt… so you're my reflection?" Bastian muttered. "Are you here to help me or just gloat?"

To his utter amazement, his reflection winked and pointed to the right. Bastian looked toward where his reflection had pointed and then back at him. Finally, he shrugged. "Well, they say when you want good advice, ask yourself. So, I guess I'll just have to trust you… or me… or yeah, whatever."

Bastian navigated the twisting corridors of the mirror maze for what felt like hours. At every junction, he turned right. Well, his reflection had just indicated to go right, so that's precisely what Bastian did. Over and over, until he started to wonder if the maze ever really ended.

"Right. I need to finish this," Bastian said, summoning more resolve and holding up the orb in front of him as he walked. "I am Sebastian Evergreen, Prince of the Spring Court, and I will protect these babies and make it through the trials if it's the last thing I do!"

As if responding to his declaration, the path ahead

began to clear. Bastian quickened his pace, his heart pounding with equal parts fear and exhilaration.

"I must be nearly there," he whispered. "I just need to stay focused."

As the mirror maze began to dissolve around him, Bastian felt the orb vanish from his hand, just as it had arrived. *Had he done something wrong? Were the twins okay?* Not receiving any answers to his questions, Bastian stumbled out of the chamber and found himself leaning against the same wall he'd found at the end of the first trial.

Bastian whooped and thrust his fist into the air. This had to mean he'd finished the second trial. Slumping to the floor, Bastian gratefully accepted the bottle of water that appeared by his side. He would have bet money Jayce had fetched it and sent it in.

CHAPTER TWENTY-EIGHT

Ellie

Ellie opened her eyes and immediately felt disoriented. She had no idea where she was or how she'd got there, but when she felt Jayce's presence beside her, she decided she didn't really care. Memories flooded back in, and Ellie reached down to cradle her belly. "Jayce?" she croaked, and his hands reached to cover hers.

"They're fine, sweetheart. I can feel their heartbeats just the same as I can feel yours. To be honest, I'm surprised you can't. But then, I only started to feel them after you passed out. Maybe you should see if you can feel them now?"

Ellie closed her eyes and focused on the place where she'd always felt Jayce's presence. Holding her breath, she searched for the signs of another presence. And then... there, two faint heartbeats almost beating as one.

"Oh, Stars, Jayce," Ellie said, releasing the breath she'd been holding and squeezing Jayce's hands. "This is exactly what I've needed. Not knowing whether... well, let's just say it's good to know."

"Yeah, I must admit it was a relief when I first felt them too. These girls sure can stress me out, and they're not even born yet."

"Oh, speaking of stress, how's Bastian? Is he—"

"He's doing great, sweetheart," Jayce interrupted her, and she bit back a smile. He'd always been good at anticipating her moods, working hard to prevent her mind from digging its way into rabbit holes. It was a habit she'd been trying to kick for a really long time." He just finished the second trial, and he looks fine. Only one more to go, and it'll be all over."

"Can I speak to him or at least see him?" Ellie asked, wanting to throw in some moral support for what the young prince was doing for them.

Jayce's eyes grew cloudy with sadness and... was it regret? Frustration? Ellie couldn't keep up with the plethora of emotions flitting across their golden depths. "Jayce? Baby, what's wrong? Is he really okay?"

Jayce breathed a huge sigh and lowered his head to kiss her belly before turning to look at her, his cheek resting where he'd kissed. "Stars, Elle. I don't even know where to start. The entire time you were unconscious, I kept wishing you'd wake up so we could talk things through like we always do. But now I'm just… I think numb is the best way to describe it. I just want to hold you and never let go."

Ellie reached down and ran her hands through his thick, dark hair. She knew exactly how he felt—Stars, it was the reason she'd been so determined to find him on Brevis. Neither of them was any good at dealing with things alone. They were a team, in every aspect of the word, and she wouldn't want it any other way.

"Sooo… does that mean I can't see or speak to Bastian? Why not?"

Jayce had closed his eyes when her hand had begun to massage his scalp. "You can see him, but only from a distance," he murmured without opening his eyes. "Apparently, the rules of the trial don't allow contact with anyone outside the trial chamber."

"Typical," Ellie huffed, not someone who ever followed the rules well. "So how can we see him then?"

"Orion has erected a clear boundary around the outside of the trial chamber. Bastian can't see us, but we can watch him inside the trials."

"Fine. Then I want to see him," Ellie had noticed that her energy levels had started to rise again. She was nowhere near back to normal, but definitely not as bad as before she'd passed out. Was it because Bastian was more than halfway through the trials? Although the why wasn't as important as the fact that it had happened.

Without another word, Jayce lifted his head and scooped her up into his arms. Carrying her to where they could look over the floor below them, she spied a forlorn-looking Bastian propped up against a wall.

"Stars preserve us, Jayce; he looks exhausted. How can we expect him to face another trial in that state?" Ellie chewed on her lip as she stared down at the previously light-hearted fae prince. He looked beaten, as if the weight of the worlds he carried had become too great a burden. Seriously, no matter how you viewed the situation, the fate of the worlds did rest on his slender young shoulders.

"Isn't there anything we can do to help him?" she asked Jayce, a tear running down her cheek. Bastian just looked so alone.

"And now you know the reason for some of the numbness I was telling you about. It's been killing me not to be able to help. But the others were right. I needed to be right where I was… with you and our babies. I shudder to think what would have happened if you'd woken up and I wasn't here."

Ellie rested her head against his chest and then snapped to attention as she watched Bastian rise and push himself away from the stone wall. This was it! He was preparing himself to go back in to face the final trial. And he was doing it for them. Humbled by the very thought of what this young man was prepared to sacrifice to keep them all safe, Ellie sent out a silent prayer to the Stars and the Fates.

Please help this young man. He has more than proven his worth already, and the realms will need a leader like him to help repair what's been broken.

CHAPTER TWENTY-NINE

Danis

*O*kay, *it was finally time!* Danis hurried over to Orion's side and touched the other man's arm. "I need to be inside the chamber with Bastian... *right now*! Look, one of the visions I had showed me inside the trial, standing beside Bastian, so it must not be against the rules. Please, Orion, it's urgent. The shield need only be down for a matter of seconds."

"You are sure this is the right path? You saw many visions. What makes you think this one is the correct path to the future we seek?" Orion gave Danis a speculative look as if he were weighing up the young fae's theory.

"Because it's the only one in which I appeared. Why give me the visions if it wasn't within my power to intervene?"

"Wise words for one so young. I will lower the shield for as long as it takes you to cross the threshold of the trial chamber. But after that, you are on your own, young seer."

Danis nodded and turned to make his way over to the shield.

"Danis Farsight?" Orion's voice stopped him in his tracks, and he turned back to face the Oracle, lifting an eyebrow in question. "I pray to all that is holy that you are right. Good luck."

Orion looked toward the shield and raised a hand. Seeing the shimmering obstacle fade away, Danis practically ran to where he'd seen Bastian standing earlier. He felt the shield slip back into place behind him and sent out a prayer to whatever deity the Oracle had sent his.

Bastian

BASTIAN STOOD at the entrance to the trial chamber for the last time. It was strange, but there appeared to be nothing on the other side but a cloudy, grey… nothingness. Fine, just one more weird illusion to deal with. He should have known by now to expect the unexpected.

Squaring his shoulders and preparing for the worst, he stepped into the nothingness. So far beyond being surprised anymore, he waited as the dizzying kaleidoscope kicked into gear, and the world around him once again shimmered before solidifying into a vast, circular chamber.

Wow... no fighting against the elements or attacks from deadly vines? So why did that not make him feel any better about the trial ahead of him?

In the middle of the vast chamber stood two concave tables resembling altars. In the closest one lay Ellie's no-longer pregnant motionless body, while the other, smaller one held the twins, their tiny bodies pulsing softly.

Bastian stared at the two altars and scratched his head. What was he supposed to do? The scene was like something out of a children's fairy tale, and apparently, no voice was going to tell him what was expected of him.

He stepped toward Ellie, about to reach out and touch her, when a familiar voice echoed around the chamber. "Bastian... stop!"

Bastian pulled his hand back as if he'd been burned and turned toward where the voice had come from.

Danis stood behind him, his silver hair gleaming in the ethereal light. His pale blue eyes, usually so serene, held a troubled intensity.

"Danis? How in the Fates did you get here?" Bastian asked, confusion clouding his features.

"How do you think I got here? The same way as you… through the door, obviously," Danis replied with a wry twist of his mouth.

"Okay, stupid question. I meant, *what* are you doing here?" Bastian couldn't hold back his grin at his friend's smart-arsed reply.

"I would have thought that was pretty obvious, too. I'm here to help you, of course," Danis replied. All previous signs of their bantering mirth disappeared, and Danis' face became deadly serious. "You know I was granted a vision of what's to come. You face an impossible choice."

Bastian's gaze flitted from Ellie to the twins and back to Danis. "Whadya mean by an impossible choice? I intend to save them all."

Danis shook his head slowly. "They are all bound by an intricate form of magic. I'm sorry, Bastian, but you can't save them all. You can either save Ellie, or you can save the twins. But not both."

"You have got to be joking," Bastian whispered, his voice cracking. "Then why did the Oracle let me believe I could save them all?

"All I can say is I'm sorry, Bas," Danis said, placing a comforting hand on his shoulder. "I don't know any of the hows or whys; I just know that the vision showed me here, standing beside you, helping you. But time is running out. You need to choose."

Bastian's mind raced, his heart torn between his duty to Jayce and his duty to the realm. Although, he already knew that having to sacrifice one to save the other would be Jayce's greatest nightmare. *Hell, it was Bastian's greatest nightmare.* "What did you see in your vision, Danis? I need you to tell me everything before I make my decision!"

Danis gave him a sad, regretful look. "I think you already know the right answer, Bas; you just don't want it to be true. The survival of the twins is crucial to the future of all the realms. We've already seen the repercussions of them not surviving. In every vision where you choose Ellie, I see darkness consuming the realm. The twins... they're important, Bastian. More than we could have imagined. They hold a power far greater than has ever been seen in all the realms. Can you honestly live with the knowledge that you failed to change the future?"

Bastian slumped to the ground, burying his face in his hands. Danis was right. None of this was about him. Besides, making the right choice meant the survival of his fated mate. That was enough... wasn't it? It would have to be.

"And what about Ellie?" he asked, his ragged voice muffled by his hands.

"I'm afraid I don't know the answer to that question, my friend. Her fate is... uncertain," Danis admitted. "But losing the twins would be the greatest catastrophe for all. Fates, it already has been. But if we have the power to stop it, we can't afford not to."

Tears stung Bastian's eyes as he looked at Ellie's

beautiful face. "Fates Danis, how can I sacrifice her? She is Jayce's… everything."

"You need to dig deep to find the strength within yourself," Danis urged. "Remember who you are, Sebastian Evergreen, Prince of the Spring Court. A leader must sometimes make painful decisions for the greater good."

Bastian closed his eyes, his chest heaving with ragged breaths. He knew without a shadow of a doubt that Danis was right. But that still didn't make the decision any easier. When he opened them again, he knew what he had to do.

Stepping toward the table that held the twins, he reached out a hand to touch them. "I… I choose the twins," he said, his voice barely above a whisper.

As soon as the words left his lips, the chamber was engulfed in a blinding light. Shielding his eyes, he felt his heart breaking even as the realisation that he'd made the right choice sunk in.

"May the Stars and the Fates forgive me," he murmured, praying that somehow, someway, Ellie would forgive him, and Jayce would understand his decision.

Stumbling out of the trial chamber, his body, heart and soul aching from the trials, Bastian immediately looked around for the Oracle.

"Ah… congratulations, young prince," Orion's melodic voice filled the room, the hint of sorrow in his words making Bastian's heart rate speed up. Surely, the

Oracle should have been a tad more excited about the end of this ridiculous debacle. "You have successfully completed the trials. But I'm afraid your journey is not yet complete."

Bastian suddenly had the overwhelming urge to punch somebody. Preferably the lying scumbag standing in front of him. "Excuse me? I've completed the damn trials. I made the ridiculous Fates-cursed choice—" His voice broke, the weight of his decision still heavy on his soul.

Orion's liquid silver eyes met Bastian's, compassion and resolve warring in their depths. "I apologise for not revealing all of the requirements at once. But you needed to complete the trials to prove you were worthy of making the decision you are now required to make. There is one more sacrifice you must make in order to remove the curse on Ellie and the twins. To save them all, you must sacrifice your bond with your fated mate."

The words hit Bastian like a physical blow. He staggered backwards, his mind struggling to accept what the Oracle was saying. "Wait," he whispered, his voice hoarse. "So, Ellie is okay? My choice didn't—"

"The sacrifice you made in the trial was a symbolic one. You needed to prove you could make the right choice if it were ever required of you. I'm sorry, but this choice is not a symbolic one," Orion said softly, his silver hair shimmering in the dim light. "Whatever decision you make now will solidify the future of all the realms. The magic requires a sacrifice of what they consider equal value. Your bond is the price they demand."

"But... you only ever get offered one fated mate," Bastian protested, his voice trembling. "How can I just give that up?"

Orion's expression remained solemn. "The choice is yours, Sebastian. But remember what hangs in the balance."

Bastian closed his eyes, his heart torn between his desire for a fated mate and his duty to Ellie, the twins, his new friends, and family. Hell, the future of all the realms hung on this one decision. Besides, if he didn't break their bond, the babies would die before they'd even drawn their first breath. At least this way, they'd both have the chance to grow up and find someone else.

And suddenly, he was angry again. The thought of the beautiful woman he'd seen in his mind with another man made his blood boil. Everything else aside, he'd done all of this to secure his bond with his fated mate. Why did he have to be the one to make all the sacrifices? Would he have even come on this ridiculous journey if he'd known he'd have to give it all up in the end? He'd never know the answer to that question, but he hoped he'd have been selfless enough to do it all anyway.

Opening his eyes, Bastian met Orion's gaze with renewed purpose.

"Fine, I'll do it," he said, his voice ragged and barely above a whisper. "Whatever it takes to save Ellie and the twins."

Orion nodded, admiration and sadness in his eyes. "Your courage is to be commended, young Prince. Your sacrifice will be responsible for the start of a whole new era."

Bastian's heart ached with an intensity he'd never experienced before. "Will she... will my fated mate, know the truth?" Bastian asked, his voice dull.

Orion's expression softened. "Yes, the twins will both be told why this happened. After all, we'll never know which of the girls could have been your mate. And who knows? Given the circumstances surrounding your loss of the fated-mate bond, it is not inconceivable that you may be recompensed for your loss. Only the Stars and the Fates know what is possible."

CHAPTER THIRTY

Orion Myst

Orion looked at the broken young man standing before him and wanted to wail at the Stars and the Fates for their cruel demands. Hadn't Bastian already done enough to help restore the prospect of a better future for all the realms? Why must the young prince's sacrifice include stripping away any hope for his future happiness? Some days, he really had to bite his tongue to hold back—

Do you wish to question our motives and decisions, old one? We would advise you to take more care when casting your recriminations.

Orion cringed as the multiple voices merged into one and entered his mind. Okay, so he was in trouble again. Not that it would be the first time. Over the thousands of years he'd endured as a sentient being, the number of times he'd risked upsetting those he'd always considered what people called gods had surpassed even his memory.

As always, I apologise for questioning your instructions, but surely you must see what prompted the recriminations.

Aahh... you have grown fond of the young, fae prince. Yes, the sacrifices he has been required to make may seem harsh, but he will have plentiful chances to redeem what he has lost. After all, he and his fated mate already had many years to wait before they could acknowledge their bond. The passing of time is filled with opportunities.

Orion's eyes widened at the implications of what the voice was not saying. If only he were free to hint at Bastian's chances of regaining what he would lose.

We will speak no more on this matter. We believe we have adequately addressed your recriminations and will assess the situation further in the future.

"Orion, one more question if I may," Bastian's voice pulled Orion back from the plane between worlds where he'd conversed with the gods. "If I do this, will it guarantee their survival, or are there more risks? Oh, and it'd be great if you could give me your word that there won't be any more surprises."

Orion tilted his head, flicking back his silver hair as he considered Bastian's request. The boy had more courage than anyone he'd previously encountered. Asking an Oracle for his word was unheard of.

"Once again, I apologise, Sebastian Evergreen," Orion's voice filled the cavernous room. "Both fate and destiny are susceptible to changes caused by the choices we make and the courage we show in the face of adversity. You must always embrace any opportunity to change what is. But the changes may not always bring the desired result."

Bastian's brow furrowed, and Orion could see the frustration building within him. "But Ellie and the babies will definitely live, right? I have noticed that your words don't always mean what they should," he pressed, and Orion couldn't hold back his smile.

Demanding his word *and* accusing him of lying. By all the gods... this pup was skating perilously close to offending him.

Still, Orion smiled at the boy in front of him. He couldn't decide whether the young fae was incredibly brave or incredibly stupid. But no matter how he felt about Bastian, the Oracle could only reveal what had been deemed acceptable by those above him. "The threads of all three burn brighter already, thanks to you, Sebastian Evergreen. Ellie and the twins now have a chance where, before, none was available."

Orion could see from the look on Bastian's face that he was about to ask for further clarification. Before the young prince could speak, Orion raised a hand to stop him, a gesture that demanded Bastian listen.

"Never forget," the Oracle said slowly, trying to imbue his words with optimism, "that destiny is derived from *all* the choices you make."

"So, there's still hope that things could change

again?" Bastian asked, the plea in his voice matching the hope in his eyes.

"Exactly," Orion nodded. "You've proven that you are more than ready for whatever challenges lie ahead. The path you are on is yours to shape, free from the limits of a predetermined fate. So... the most important lesson to be learned is that you must never stop trying."

Bastian

"BASTIAN! Please tell me you're not even considering giving up the bond?" Ellie called out in a surprisingly strong yet shaky voice. "It's your future... yours and one of my daughter's. Damnit... It's everything you've fought for!" She turned her eyes toward the Oracle. "How can this even be fair?"

Bastian hadn't even realised Ellie and Jayce were in the room. He looked over to see Ellie in Jayce's arms, tears streaming down her face. And by the look on Jayce's face, he wasn't happy about any of it either.

"Wait, what the hell is going on here?" Jayce asked, his gravelly voice tight with emotion. "Why would

Bastian need to give up his mate bond? It has nothing to do with the cure."

With his mind spinning from the choices he'd been forced to make that day, Bastian suddenly wished they'd all just leave him alone. But the reality of Ellie's words had cut into him like a knife. A fated mate bond was so much more than just finding the person you were meant to be with. It was… everything. He knew that its loss would devastate his future, but still his choices must remain the same.

Orion turned his liquid silver eyes upon them all. "I also wish that were true. But the power released when the bond is broken will add fuel to the magic needed to heal the twins and restore balance. It is a sacrifice of the highest order."

Bastian looked at Ellie and Jayce and sighed. "So, there's definitely no other way?" Bastian asked Orion, a tinge of desperation in his words.

The Oracle's expression remained impassive. "The paths of fate may be many, young prince. But at this moment in time, no other choice is available to you. You know what hangs in the balance."

Bastian closed his eyes, his thoughts bombarded by the brief vision of the girls grown up and breathtakingly beautiful. He almost wished he'd never had the vision, would never know what he'd come so close to finding. And even though he knew it was ridiculous to pine for something you never had, Bastian already felt like he was giving up a part of himself.

Okay, it was time to stop railing against the inevitable. It didn't matter that what he was being asked to do sucked big time. Just thinking of all the people in the realms depending on him, Bastian knew what he had to do. This was about so much more than his happiness.

"I have to do this, guys. I already informed the Oracle of my choice," he said, his voice sounding harsh in the silence.

Orion nodded, and Bastian didn't miss the sadness in his eyes. "You have shown great courage and fortitude today, young prince. You should know that your sacrifice will change the future in ways we can't even imagine."

As the reality of his decision settled in, the ache in Bastian's chest became almost unbearable. He would save Ellie and the twins, but at what cost? The thought of never feeling that special connection only experienced between fated mates threatened to overwhelm him.

Bastian only nodded, clinging to that small glimmer of hope as he prepared to face a future that would be forever changed by a cruel twist of fate.

CHAPTER THIRTY-ONE

Bastian

Bastian had lost count of the number of times his heart had thundered in his chest in that one day. He was starting to think he'd be better off *without* the troublesome organ. What with having to put up with it breaking, aching, thundering and almost stopping on a regular basis, the stupid thing had practically become a hindrance more than a help. Okay, so maybe he needed it to continue to pump so he stayed alive, but still…

Yep, it was official. Bastian Evergreen, Prince of the Fae Spring Court, had completely lost his mind. *I mean, who ponders the pros and cons of needing a heart while waiting for some magical ritual to remove a curse and break a bond to begin?* He looked around at the stark walls of the Ritual Chamber, longing to be anywhere but there.

Orion's timeless eyes seemed to pierce his very soul. "Are you ready, young prince? The path before you is not an easy one. The ritual, once started, cannot be reversed."

"I'm ready," Bastian said, his voice barely above a whisper. *I'm so ready for it all to be over.* He knew now, without a doubt, that he was making the only choice that was ever possible. He would move mountains for Ellie and the two beautiful baby girls she carried. Hey, he'd even wrestle with the Fates if it was necessary.

A ghost of a smile played at Orion's lips as he nodded. "Excellent. But before we start, I must tell you that if the removal of the curse is successful, you will each be transported back to the entrance to the Aqueous Flow from which you came to Brevis. Now, it is time to begin."

The Oracle glided to the centre of the chamber—*yes, that's right, he glided, since he was now wearing elaborate flowing robes that shimmered in the eerie half-light.* He raised his arms, and Bastian wondered if everyone else in the room was holding their breath in anticipation like he was.

Bastian's heart clenched—*yep, that was another annoying thing it did on a regular basis. Okay, enough with the nervous quips. It was time to get serious again. This was it. There was no turning back after whatever was about to happen next.*

Orion's powerful voice echoed off the walls, sending shivers down Bastian's spine. The ancient words caused magic to pulse with raw energy in the air around them.

As the chanting began to echo off the walls, the volume grew in intensity. As if the words had created a link to his body, a tugging sensation grew deep within Bastian's chest. He knew in an instant that it was the fated mate bond, the very essence of his connection starting to unravel. Tears pricked at the corners of his eyes, but he blinked them away. This was no time to feel sorry for himself. He needed to stay strong...

The air crackled with arcane energy as the Oracle's chant seemed to reach inside Bastian's chest, as if searching for the bond to be sacrificed. Bastian's world narrowed to a pinpoint of light, his entire being focused on what was being dragged from his body.

He looked over to where Ellie lay upon the stone altar, her vibrant features drawn and pale, her face etched with lines of pain.

"Bastian," she whispered when she saw him, her voice barely audible over Orion's chanting. "I'm so sorry. The babies... please..."

Bastian's heart constricted at the vulnerability in her plea. He stepped closer, his hand hovering just above hers. "It's okay, Ellie. This will save you all."

A single tear slid down Ellie's cheek as she managed a weak smile. "Thank you," she breathed.

A low growl pulled Bastian's attention to where Jayce stood rigid, his muscular frame taut with tension, his knuckles white from his tightly clenched fists. Bastian could almost feel the storm of emotions raging beneath the dragon shifter's controlled exterior.

"What if this doesn't work?" Jayce muttered, more to himself than anyone else. Then he grabbed fistfuls of his own hair and pulled. "No, I need to stop thinking like that… it has to work."

Bastian was relieved to see Danis move closer to Jayce, placing a hand on the dragon shifter's shoulder as if to reassure him. "Have faith, my friend," Danis murmured, his concerned eyes flicking between Jayce and the scene unfolding before them. "The power of love will always defeat the power of evil."

Jayce sucked in a long, slow breath. "And what if it's not enough?"

Danis' gaze flickered briefly to Jayce, his eyes pools of sadness. "Then we'll face whatever happens together."

Ellie's gasp pulled Bastian's attention back to where she lay. Her eyes, wide with a mix of hope and fear, locked onto Jayce's. Bastian tried to push down the pang of jealousy that ripped through him at the evidence of a bond he'd never experience.

"Jayce? Whatever happens," Ellie whispered, her voice stronger now, fueled by determination, "know that I love you, my gorgeous dragon."

A sudden palpable shift in the atmosphere made the hairs on Bastian's arms stand on end. The air crackled with intensity as swirls of iridescent light danced around them, casting ethereal shadows across the stone walls of the Fae Castle. The space pulsed with an otherworldly energy while ribbons of colour wove intricate patterns overhead.

Bastian kept his eyes fixed on Ellie's prone form. The weight of what he was doing pressed heavily upon him, but he was way past hesitating or questioning his decisions.

"It is time, Sebastian Evergreen," the Oracle announced, his melodic voice tinged with determination.

Bastian moved to stand closer to Ellie, placing his trembling hands over her heart. The magic within him surged, and he had to fight the urge to step away. *Holy Fates... his magic had never felt so intense.* Closing his eyes, Bastian drew in a deep breath, centering himself for what he knew was to come.

"I won't let you or your babies down, Ellie," he whispered, his soft words meant for her ears alone. "Just know that I'll do whatever it takes."

Ellie's hand found his, squeezing gently. "Their names are Angel and Sera, short for Seraphim," she replied, her voice as soft as his.

Bastian smiled down at the beautiful woman who had placed her unconditional trust in him. "And perfect names they are too." He was suddenly overcome by a sense of clarity. This all just felt so right. No matter the cost, this was what he was meant to do.

With one last look at his friends—Jayce's tense nod, Danis' encouraging smile—Bastian closed his eyes once more. He focused inward, channelling every ounce of his fae magic into breaking the curse that threatened everything they held dear.

Bastian's body tensed, his jaw clenching as the first wave of pain crashed into him, and a sensation like that of molten lava began to course through his veins, searing every nerve ending. He gritted his teeth, refusing to cry out.

I'm okay. It's only pain, and it's only temporary. The words became his mantra as he continued to pour his magic into Ellie. Then, he felt the fated mate bond being stretched, thinning as if it had almost reached its limit. And when it finally snapped, the loss was like a piece of his soul had been torn away. Even so he pushed on.

Ellie

"ELLIE," Bastian gasped, his voice strained. "Can you feel it working?"

As if she'd been poked by a cattle prod, Ellie's back arched of its own accord, a strangled gasp escaping her lips. But when warmth began to flood into her body, chasing away the icy tendrils of the curse, it was like stepping into the sunlight after an eternity of darkness.

"Yes," she breathed, a sense of wonder momentarily masking the pain. "Oh, Bastian, I can feel it. But you're hurting—"

Bastian managed a weak smile, sweat beading on his brow. "Don't worry about me. Focus on the light, Elle. You need to let it in."

As the curse continued to unravel, Ellie's chest ached with a bittersweet sadness. She hated that this boy was suffering because of her. Sure, she knew that none of this was her fault, nor had she asked him to make such a devastating sacrifice. But none of that made it any easier to see the torment in Bastian's silver eyes.

"Stars, Bastian. I am so sorry this is happening to you... I never expected it to be so hard..." she whispered, tears streaming down her cheeks.

Bastian shook his head, his resolve unwavering despite the excruciating pain. "Never apologise for this. Knowing you and the babies will be safe makes it all worth it."

Ellie's eyes moved to Jayce. He stood rigid, his fists clenched at his sides as he watched the ritual unfold. The air in the Castle's chamber crackled with energy, but the tension coming off Jayce's body rivalled the magical currents swirling around them.

"I love you, Elle," Jayce whispered, his voice barely audible over the hum of magic. Then his face contorted when Ellie was unable to hide the surge of pain knifing into her body.

CHAPTER THIRTY-TWO

Jayce

Jayce felt a new surge of gratitude and guilt wash over him as he watched Bastian struggle to hide the agony he was experiencing. The young fae's sacrifice had gone way above and beyond any of their expectations.

Okay, so it's time I got my act together and at least tried to stop looking like I was ready to claw my own eyes out. Everything is fine. Yep, just fine!

"How much longer?" The question had slipped from his lips before he could stop it, and he groaned. *Yeah, way to go, Dufus. Like asking dumb questions would help anyone.*

Danis, who still stood beside him, gave him an understanding smile. "I don't think anyone really knows, Jayce," he replied softly. "Just gotta trust in the process, I guess."

Jayce nodded, swallowing hard. "Yeah, I'm trying. It's just... seeing them both in pain..."

"I know what you mean. But seeing us stressed won't help them. They need to see our strength so they can feed from it and increase their own," Danis murmured, his eyes straying back to Bastian and Ellie.

"Stars, man. That was some incredibly philosophical shit right there. I'd never have guessed you had that kind of insight in you."

All joviality vanished as he watched Ellie arch her back again, followed by a moan as another wave of magic pulsed through the room. Jayce's resolve not to go to her was stretched to the breaking point. "Bastian," he called out, his voice thick with emotion. "You're doing great, son. Just keep doing what you're doing for as long as you can. And just know that you have our undying love and gratitude."

Bastian's silver eyes flickered open, meeting Jayce's gaze. A ghost of a smile crossed his face before he returned his focus to Ellie.

Jayce felt his chest tighten, the weight of Bastian's sacrifice settling heavily on his shoulders. How the hell could he ever repay the debt he owed this selfless young fae prince?

As if sensing his turmoil, Danis spoke again. "This is not a debt to be repaid, my friend. What is happening here is love in its purest form."

Jayce turned to look at the elf, struck by the depth of understanding in his eyes. "How can you be so calm?" he asked, a little envious of Danis' serene demeanour.

Danis smiled softly. "Because I can feel the strength of the love flowing all around us. And I just know that everything is going to be fine."

With those words, Jayce felt a flicker of hope ignite in his chest. He straightened his shoulders, drawing on an inner strength he hadn't known he possessed.

"You're right," he said, his voice steady. "We'll get through this. All of us… together."

Having finally put his inner demons to rest, for now, at least, Jayce straightened his shoulders and stood tall, a silent custodian offering his unwavering support. His emotions threatened to overwhelm him, but he refused to let them. For Ellie, for Bastian, for the future of their unusual family, he would be the pillar they all so desperately needed.

The air in the ritual chamber crackled with raw energy, a colourful display of dazzling light swirling over and around Ellie and Bastian. Even the stones beneath their feet began to hum with power, resonating with Orion's otherworldly chanting.

Ellie

ELLIE'S BREATH caught in her throat as the curse's grip continued to loosen. "Holy Stars in the heavens, Bastian. It's... it's working," she whispered, her voice barely carrying over the frenzied magical display.

Bastian nodded without opening his eyes, his hands still placed steadily over her heart. "Just... a bit… more," he gritted out, his face contorted with the effort and pain.

Suddenly, the swirling lights blended into a blinding flash, and Ellie felt the magic surge before something inside her seemed to snap, like a rubber band stretched too tight. The relief was instant. The darkness she'd felt growing inside her began to recede, taking with it the crushing burden she'd been carrying, and she felt lighter than air.

"I can breathe again!" Ellie gasped, her eyes flying open. She gulped in the clean, fresh air, basking in the sensation of breathing freely for the first time in what felt like ages. "Bastian, you did it!"

As the euphoric glow began to fade, Ellie's gaze locked onto Bastian's pain-ravaged face. The joy of no longer feeling the curse's dark taint warred with the reality of what the young prince had sacrificed. "Oh Bastian, I'm so… so sorry. I... I don't know how I'll ever thank you," she said, her voice heavy with emotion.

Bastian managed a sad smile. "Seeing you and the

babies safe is all the thanks I need," he replied, his slightly slurred words evidence of his exhaustion.

Ellie reached out, grasping his hand. "But your bond... Bastian, I never wanted you to lose that. Not for me."

"It was my choice," Bastian said, his voice slightly stronger, though Ellie could see the pain flickering in his eyes. "One I'd make again in a heartbeat."

Overwhelmed, Ellie reached out to pull him into a tight embrace. "Thank you," she whispered, tears spilling down her cheeks. "For everything."

Bastian

BASTIAN FELT the last tendrils of his fated mate bond slip away as Ellie's arms reached out to encircle him. Suddenly, the loss hit him like a physical blow, and he crumpled to the ground, his legs no longer able to support him.

"Bastian!" Ellie cried out, her voice tinged with alarm.

Bastian pressed his palms against the cool stone floor, trying to anchor himself as waves of dizziness washed over him. The void where his bond had been yawned impossibly wide, threatening to swallow him whole.

"I'm... I'm all right," Bastian managed, though his voice trembled. He closed his eyes, drawing in a shaky breath. "It's just... well, I feel kind of empty inside."

The hollowness was almost unbearable, but Bastian clung to the knowledge that he had made the only possible choice. His loss had saved Ellie and her unborn children. That knowledge helped him to stay afloat, even as he felt adrift in a sea of loss.

Across the ritual space, Jayce rushed to Ellie's side. His piercing honey-gold eyes shone with relief, his love almost heart-wrenching in its intensity, as he gathered Ellie into his arms.

"My love," he murmured, pressing his forehead to hers. "Is it really gone? All of it?"

Ellie nodded, her own eyes brimming with tears. "Thanks to Bastian," she whispered. "But oh, Jayce, the cost..."

"Shh," Jayce soothed, pushing the tendrils of sweat-soaked hair off her face. "We'll find a way to thank Bastian for what he's done... I promise." His gaze flickered to Bastian, a mix of gratitude and concern etched on his already ravaged features. Then the world around them dissolved, and he and Danis were back inside the Fae Castle, looking exactly as it had when they left.

Bastian still lay in the same position he'd been in back in the trial chamber, and didn't have the energy, or the will, to rise any more now than he'd had then. In fact, if he were honest, he wanted nothing more than to curl into a ball and cry. What was the point of anything anymore?

He was snapped out of his morbid thoughts when the weight of Danis' gentle hand fell onto his shoulder. He looked up to find his best friend kneeling beside him, the seer's silver-blue eyes a swirling pool of concern and understanding.

"Breathe, my friend," Danis said softly. "The worst is finally over."

Bastian shook his head, leaning into Danis' steadying grip. "I'm not so sure about that, Dan. It feels like... like a huge part of me is gone," he confessed,

Danis squeezed his shoulder. "I know it was a terrible sacrifice, Bas. But I promise I'll always be here for you whenever you need me."

Danis' words warmed Bastian's heart, easing the ache of loss ever so slightly. He managed a wan smile. "Thank you. But I don't think you fully understand what's happened. When the bond was sucked out, so was my magic and therefore my link to The Spring

Court. Everything I was... It's all gone, Danis. There's nothing left."

"Wait... what? Did the Oracle mention that anything like this might happen?" Danis asked, panic replacing all previous emotions.

"Nope... and it's not like I can ask him about it now, right?"

"Maybe if we go meet up with Ellie and Jayce in the Dragon Realm, they might know how to fix it."

And what if it's beyond fixing? He didn't say the words out loud, his friend was already worried enough.

"Sounds like a plan," Bastian said, trying to put on a brave front. "We might need to get your Mum to teleport us to the Dragon Council Chambers, though. Hopefully, she's been there before. I know someone there who should be able to get us to Jayce's castle."

With a deep breath, Bastian squared his shoulders, preparing to face whatever challenges lay ahead. The journey back to reality—and an uncertain future—had begun.

CHAPTER THIRTY-THREE

Jayce

Jayce stepped away from the pool that led to the Aqueous Flow and left the Dragon Council meeting room at a run. He ignored the looks from other council members as he raced for the front door, morphing into his dragon form and leaping into the sky just as he heard Rhett's voice from the doorway.

"Jayce? What the hell, man? Where are you—" He'd just have to hope that Rhett figured out where he was going and followed him if he wanted answers.

His heart soared when he caught sight of Ellie standing in the courtyard of Raythawn Castle waiting for him. He couldn't wait to land, pull her into his arms, and never let go. How come nobody ever listened to him when he said bad things happened when they were apart? Well, one thing was for sure. The Dragon Realm would freeze over before it happened again.

Jayce landed, morphed, and had Ellie in his arms before he'd even taken a breath. For once, not even the size of her swollen belly coming between them bothered him. And from the way Ellie was crushing herself against him, she was beyond caring, too.

"Home sweet, glorious, amazing home," Ellie murmured, her voice wavering slightly.

Jayce chuckled. "So, can I take that to mean you're happy to be home then?"

"Understatement of the century, my love," Ellie replied.

"Well, I suppose we should go in and tell them we're home. Something tells me they'll all be demanding the details of what happened."

Ellie groaned and lifted her face to look into his eyes. "Wait… so you're saying I can't just go inside, say hello, and then go to bed?"

Jayce threw back his head and laughed. "Do you honestly believe your mother would let that happen? She'll be chafing at the bit to know everything."

"Fine," Ellie was obviously trying to look like she was *huffing* over the whole thing, but he saw the mischief dancing in her eyes. "They can have me for like half an hour, and then I'm going to bed. And *you* will be joining me. Don't even try to argue with me. I'm a ridiculously hormonal pregnant woman who's been to hell and back. Which means that what anyone else wants can just wait!"

Jayce was still grinning as he turned them toward the entrance to the castle. He pitied anyone who tried to take on his wife in this mood.

They were almost at the door when a familiar voice called out from behind them.

"Yeah, don't worry about me. I was fine with being interrogated by a witch ready to tear my head off if I didn't reveal your whereabouts. That's what best friends are for, right?"

Jayce turned to find Rhett marching towards them, with Bastian and Danis close behind him.

"Oh, and you're also welcome that I brought your new friends here to find you, too." Rhett finally reached them and pulled him into a bro-hug. "Plus, I've been worried sick about you for the last three days," Rhett said soft enough for Jayce's ears only.

"Did you say three days? How the hell have we been gone that long? I don't remember spending even one night there."

Ellie just groaned again. "No wonder I'm so tired. How did we miss all that time passing?"

Danis had caught up and stood beside Rhett. "Are you seriously questioning the workings of time after what we just went through? Fates, we've been too busy jumping around between centuries to miss a few days."

They all laughed at the irony of Danis' statement, except Rhett, who just looked at them all as if they'd lost their minds. Not that he'd have been too far off the mark a few hours ago.

Jayce's heart clenched at the sight of Bastian appearing to cower behind Danis, so unlike the young prince he'd first met. Bastian looked… broken. In fact, he looked even worse than the last time he'd seen him. *What the Stars had happened between now and then?*

"Bastian? You okay, son?" Jayce asked, and wanted to bite off his tongue as Bastian winced at the term of endearment he'd used. After what this boy had lost in the last twenty-four hours, or however long it had been, addressing him as *son* must have felt like having salt rubbed into his wound.

"Yeah… about that," Danis cut in before Bastian could answer. "We might need to all sit down and have a quiet talk when we get a minute."

"Why? What's wrong? Bastian, what's he—" Ellie's frantic questions were interrupted by Jayce's soothing voice.

"Calm down, sweetheart. I'm sure if something urgent was wrong, Danis wouldn't have suggested it could wait. Am I right, boys?"

Both the young fae boys nodded, and Jayce felt the tension leave Ellie's body. Honestly, it was like every time they thought their problems had been dealt with, another problem would slide out from under the previous one and present a new one. Jayce was mentally and physically exhausted, and they still had to deal with the family members waiting for them inside.

"Okay, I think it might be best if we went inside and let them all know we're fine. Telling them everything that's happened since we left is going to take a while. Bastian? Danis? You guys up to meeting the family right now, or I can have a couple of the guest rooms made up and you can have a rest?"

Danis and Bastian shared a look, and then both smiled and nodded. "I think we could probably manage a few introductions before we slink away and hide," Danis said, linking arms with his best friend. "So, let's get it over with then, shall we?"

They all turned and headed inside the castle, each trying to hide their weariness behind welcoming smiles.

Bastian

OKAY, *it was way past time to squash the poor-me persona back into its box and get on with it!* He and all his new family and friends had survived the ordeals they'd faced on Brevis, and it was time to start being grateful for what they'd accomplished instead of wallowing in self-pity. He didn't even know if the loss of his magic and bond with the Spring Court was permanent, or just a temporary thing resulting from giving too much in the ritual.

Even as he berated himself, Bastian couldn't help admiring Jayce's ancestral home. From the moment they stepped inside the massive front doors, a welcoming ambience seemed to surround his weary body. They had reached the entry to a large lounge-room when two women came flying through the doors, one pulling Jayce into her arms while the other carefully hugged Ellie.

"Oh, praise the Stars, you're both alright. We have been beside ourselves with worry, not knowing whether you were… ahem, well, it's just wonderful to see you both home and safe," the woman holding Ellie babbled, who looked so much like Ellie she had to be her mother.

"What she said," the other woman laughed, reaching for Ellie's hand and giving her an adoring smile.

The one he had assumed was Ellie's mum turned her attention to him and Danis. "And I'm assuming one of you is the fae prince who came and lured Jayce away in the middle of the night?"

Bastian broke into the first genuine smile he'd felt for a while and bowed. He liked this outspoken, family-oriented woman already. "That would be me. I am Prince Sebastian Evergreen, heir to the Spring Court of the Fae Realm. And this is my best friend, Danis Farsight, a phenomenal seer of the Spring Court. I am pleased to make your acquaintance, fair ladies, and I apologise for my role in coercing Jayce to join me on a brief but crucial trip to Brevis."

Everyone in the room laughed at Bastian's formal but cheeky introduction. "Well met, Prince Sebastian. I am Yvette Fiora, Ellie's mother, and this is Iridia Raythawn, Jayce's mother."

All attention flew to Jayce as he cleared his throat, raised his arms and rolled his eyes. "Oh, for Stars sake. Can we please move past the ridiculous formalities and at least sit down somewhere comfortable? Ellie is practically dead on her feet, and the rest of us aren't far behind her."

Jayce's mother, Iridia, stepped back from Jayce and immediately began to wring her hands. "Oh, I'm so sorry. How rude of me. Please, come sit down while I arrange for a meal to be set up in the dining room. I'm sure you all must be starving as well."

Bastian actually chuckled at the sound of a tummy rumbling. He had no idea whose stomach it came from, but he could definitely relate to their predicament. He couldn't even remember the last time he'd eaten. He sat on a comfortable lounge next to Danis, closing his eyes and breathing out a sigh of relief as he realised that he also couldn't remember the last time he'd been either comfortable or relaxed.

Trying to ignore the sensation of being watched, he finally opened his eyes and looked straight into Ellie's emerald green ones. Her worried frown and the concern in her eyes only served to make him even more determined to shrug off the cloud of self-pity under which he'd been buried.

Are you okay? Ellie mouthed from across the room.

I'm fine. Stop worrying, Bastian mouthed back, summoning a smile, and throwing her a wink—yet another thing he couldn't remember doing recently.

Right, no more letting Mr Sadsack out in public. From now on, *that persona* would be limited to when he was alone.

CHAPTER THIRTY-FOUR

Ellie

Stars, it was good to be home. Everything in her world was finally back to normal. Except, of course, for Bastian. Every time she thought about him, she was flooded with guilt and sadness for what the young fae prince had sacrificed.

Trying to observe Bastian surreptitiously from the other side of the room, she was convinced that something else had happened since the ritual. He looked... defeated. It was the only word that aptly described him as he sat quietly beside Danis.

Jayce, I think something else is going on with Bastian. He looks even worse than when we all left Brevis.

Well, if there is, I'm sure he'll tell us about it when he gets the chance. Now will you please stop stressing and just relax.

I'm sure our baby girls could do with a break from all the trauma.

Iridia re-entered the room with a huge smile on her face. "Right. It's time for some eating and talking. Because I'm worried that Yvette and I may burst if we don't know everything soon."

"That makes three of us," Rhett said, throwing a dirty look in hers and Jayce's direction. "I am the best friend here, remember?

They all moved quietly to the dining room and sat around the ornate table covered in more food than Ellie could ever remember seeing in one place. The kitchen staff had performed miracles—obviously aided by a copious amount of magic—with such short notice.

Mum clinked a spoon against her wine glass and smiled at them all. "Okay, so I understand that you are probably all starving, so we'll allow you the first five minutes to assuage the worst of it. After that, I don't care who starts, but detailed explanations will be forthcoming."

"Mum!" Ellie hissed in mock horror, biting back the giggle her mother's words had prompted. "Bossy much?"

Ellie was surprised to see that her mother was actually blushing and looking down at her plate. "Sorry huni. It's been an incredibly stressful three days. I know that's nothing compared to what you have all obviously been through, but waiting has always made me feel like my insides are being eaten away."

"You know what?" Danis said, putting down his knife and fork and smiling at her mum. "I think it might be best if we tag-team telling the story. So, I'll start while everyone continues to eat, and then we can take it in turns to each tell our own sides of the story. Does that sound okay?"

Ellie sighed in relief as Danis managed to placate everyone present. It wasn't the first time he'd stepped up and taken control of a tense situation, and Ellie threw him a grateful smile. Danis just nodded and began to speak.

"So, I guess the best place to start is when I received a vision related to the prophecy." As he proceeded to reveal the details of what he'd seen, a tense silence descended upon everyone at the table. For those who'd been involved, it was the start of having to relive what they'd endured, while those not involved seemed to just sit in a stunned silence.

Yeah, she was pretty sure that her own imagination could never have even come close to envisaging what they'd lived through. Hell, Ellie had been there and was still struggling to believe some of the crap they'd dealt with.

Once Danis had finished relating everything from his vision, Bastian stepped up to tell them about what the old Priestess had revealed, how he'd found Jayce, and Danis' mother opening the entrance to Brevis. As soon as he finished, Jayce jumped in from where he'd met Bastian to when he'd heard Ellie's voice in his head.

Ellie had sat through the entire ordeal, learning a few things she hadn't known about before she arrived on Brevis. She knew she'd be up next, and the thought of saying everything out loud made her want to throw up. Although she remembered hearing once that talking about trauma experienced sometimes helped in the healing process. Besides, her mum, Iridia and Rhett deserved to know what had happened to them, and what they'd learned about the future.

Elle baby... you okay? Jayce's soothing voice inside her head pulled her from her thoughts, and she realised that everyone was looking at her with worried frowns. *Shit... how long had I been off in la-la land?*

"So I'm assuming it must be my turn then? Sorry, I got a bit side-tracked. Right, so I guess I'll start from the first time I heard the babies' voices in my head."

"The first time?" Her mum hissed, her face pale. "When—"

Ellie held up her hand and smiled at her mother. "Sorry Mum, but I need to get this over with. I promise you'll know everything by the time I'm finished. Then, if anyone has any questions, we'll go from there."

Sucking in a deep breath, and squeezing Jayce's hand under the table, she started to speak.

Bastian

BY THE TIME their show and tell session was over, Bastian was exhausted. He knew his friends would be the same, so decided to put off the chat they'd planned to have before retiring to their rooms. It wasn't like he expected there to be a solution to his problem, so why rush giving Ellie and Jayce just another thing to worry about. They had more than enough on their plates, and he hated that they felt indebted to him for his sacrifice. Telling them it had cost him not only his fated mate, but his magic and claim to the throne as well would be cruel.

Noticing the lull in the conversation around the table, Bastian stood and looked at Jayce. "Would anyone mind if I retired now? Sorry, but I am absolutely beat."

The sympathetic looks from everyone at the table almost brought him undone. He needed to get away from all of this and just have some time alone.

Everyone jumped to their feet and started to discuss what guest rooms were available. His head had begun to pound, and his legs felt like jelly. For Fate's sake, he didn't need the fuss, just somewhere to lie down.

He felt a hand slip into his, and he realised Ellie was beside him. She gave him a soft smile and gently pulled him from the room.

"Sorry Bastian, I could see how over everything you were, and I know exactly which room you need to be in. Let's go before they notice we're missing."

Bastian just nodded, unable to speak past the lump in his throat due to Ellie's kindness. They walked in silence until they reached a door which Ellie pushed open. The room was opulent, similar to any of the guest rooms in the Spring Court Palace. But it was the bed that called to him like a siren. He turned to Ellie, unsure what he wanted to say. But she simply placed a finger on his lips and kissed his cheek.

"Sleep well, my prince. Tomorrow will be soon enough to deal with whatever it is." Then she turned and left the room, the door closing silently behind her. And he was alone. Wasn't that what he'd wanted? It was the first time he'd been alone since Danis had entered his room and tipped his entire life upside down.

He looked down at himself and noticed for the first time how bad he looked. Fates… he'd presented himself to Ellie and Jayce's families looking like this? Wow. The fact that he found himself not caring told him more than anything else how much the past few days had changed him. The old Bastian would never have considered even leaving his rooms in this state. But somehow, none of that mattered any more. It was all just stuff.

Knowing he should have a shower but too tired to care, he stripped off the clothes he'd been wearing and slipped under the cool sheets of the king-size bed. With everything that had happened swirling around in his head, he was sure he'd never sleep. But sleep he did.

CHAPTER THIRTY-FIVE

Danis

Danis watched his friend leave the dining room with Ellie and sagged back in his chair, letting his eyes close for just a minute. He didn't know what to do or how to help Bastian, and it was driving him nuts. He'd told Ellie and Jayce they'd discuss Bastian's new problem together, but Danis was starting to think it would be better if he just told Jayce himself. The dragon shifter could then decide what they should do, who they should speak to and whether anyone else needed to know.

Danis opened his eyes to find Jayce already looking at him. As if they'd both come to the same conclusion, Jayce nodded toward the outside patio and headed out. Without another thought, Danis followed him.

"Jayce—" Danis said, as soon as he stepped out of the doorway

"Danis—" Jayce said at the same time. They both chuckled and began to move toward where a bench seat sat on the far side of the patio. "Okay, you go first," Jayce said.

"Honestly? I don't know what to say or do. Would you mind if whatever I say is kept between you and me for the time being?"

"No problem at all, my friend. Now, can you please tell me what has happened since we left Brevis?"

"Bastian has lost his magic and all previous ties to the Spring Court," Danis blurted, relieved to be able to share the burden of his secret with someone else.

Jayce just stared at him, as if waiting for him to say something else. But Danis just shook his head. He watched the anger boil in Jayce, his eyes turning black. "Stars Danis. I can't believe this is happening. Haven't they taken enough from him already? Do we even know whether it's temporary or permanent?"

"We know nothing. And it's not like we can ask the Oracle. It's killing me that I can't do anything to help him." Danis felt the tears welling in his eyes, and he brushed them away furiously. "How can the Fates be so cruel? What has he ever done to deserve any of this?"

"Sooo... when did he realise it was gone?" Jayce asked, his eyes slowly returning to normal.

"I'm pretty sure it wasn't until we landed back in

the Fae Realm. Or at least, that's when he told me about it."

"Is there anyone in the Fae Realm you trust enough to ask for help? Someone who might know more about Fae Magic?"

"I'm sure Danis would say that would be me," a familiar woman's voice said from the shadows behind them.

Danis spun around to find his mother emerging from where she'd been hidden. "Mum? You were supposed to go straight back home. What are you doing here?"

"Did you honestly believe I would leave you here knowing Bastian had lost the use of his magic?" Bella Farsight said with a smile. "Yes, I know you told me that he was just too weak from removing the curse to portal you here, but seriously Danis? Do I really look that stupid?"

Danis was unable to do anything but stare at his mother open-mouthed. She'd risked becoming involved in what would be labelled treason against the crown if it ever came to light. He finally closed his mouth, sighed, and turned to Jayce.

"Mother, this is Jayce Raythawn, Head of the Dragon Council. And this, Jayce, is my mother, Bella Farsight, Seer for the King of the Spring Court."

"It is a pleasure to meet the woman who raised such a remarkable young man. Well met, Bella Farsight,"

Jayce replied, and Danis nearly fell over when Jayce actually bowed to his mother.

"Thank you for your kind words," Bella said with a blush. "But we need to get on with what we are all here for. I fear we won't be alone much longer, and I'm assuming that what we're discussing is not public knowledge?"

"Was it wrong of me to tell Jayce without Bastian's knowledge?" Danis asked, fearing his mother would be disappointed in him.

"No, Danis. You did exactly what was necessary, as I'm sure Jayce will agree. Now, what exactly has happened, and what was the cause?"

Danis quickly filled his mother in on what had happened on Brevis and how it had affected Bastian. Bella's dark frown when he'd finished was not a good sign.

"Well, from what I know of the legends surrounding the Oracle, he would not have withheld the knowledge from Bastian if the loss was to be permanent. His sacrifice of his fated mate was the price demanded, and it was paid in full. So this loss has to be temporary. I know of a few spells that may speed up his recovery, but we still won't know when it will be restored."

"Oh, thank you, Mum. I was—" Danis began, feeling as if the weight of the world had been lifted off his shoulders.

"Wait, Danis. Don't thank me yet. That only

addresses *one* of Bastian's problems. I fear the other will be much harder to fix. While it's not unusual for the blood bond to the Spring Court to weaken when the prince is far from home, Bastian cannot return to the Spring Court until the ties are fully restored. The King currently believes you and Bastian are in the Summer Court with Harris, but we don't know how long he'll allow Bastian to be away from Court."

"If I may interrupt," Jayce said, his brow still furrowed. "I think it might be best if we deal with what we can now. I'm sure what we've discussed, and Bella's spells, will help Bastian to cope for now. Bastian and Danis are welcome to stay with us as long as they want, and if you, Bella, could keep us informed about the King's needs where Bastian is concerned, we can only hope that Bastian can claw his way back from the dark place he's currently in."

CHAPTER THIRTY-SIX

Jayce

*J*ayce's inner battle over whether to share with Ellie what he'd learned from Danis was brought to an abrupt halt when Ellie herself stepped out the door onto the patio, the look on her face telling him his decision had been made for him.

"Hey, sweetheart. We were just wondering where you were. Is Bastian okay?" Jayce asked as he attempted to pull her into his arms.

"Seriously? You expect me to believe you were just out here discussing the weather and waiting for me to join you? Stars Jayce, will you never learn that keeping secrets from me does not end well. Like, ever!"

Jayce froze at the sound of Bella's chuckle. Ellie did not respond well to anyone laughing when she was in this mood. "You must be Ellie, the mother of the twins I've heard so much about. Thank the Fates Bastian was able to remove the curse, and you are all looking so well. Oh, and I am Bella Farsight, Danis' mother, in case you were wondering."

Ellie's expression was priceless as she took in the beautiful woman standing before her. Like all fae, Jayce was quickly learning, Bella was achingly beautiful and looked like what he'd always imagined a goddess would. The smile she was giving Ellie was blindingly perfect, and Elle just stared.

"Sorry, honey," Jayce said, slipping an arm around her waist. "This wasn't a planned meeting, and we weren't trying to hide anything from you. In fact, Danis and I came out to get some fresh air, and Bella appeared out of nowhere."

Ellie finally shook herself out of her stupor and looked at Danis. "Does this mean you already told Jayce what's wrong with Bastian?" she asked, giving Danis a disappointed look. Danis blushed and looked down at his shoes. Jayce knew all too well how it felt to get one of those looks from Ellie.

"I just… I didn't know what to do. Bastian and I had decided to tell you all together, but when I saw the state he was in when you led him upstairs, I knew I had to do something. So… I asked Jayce for help. I'm sorry, Ellie. I didn't mean to—"

Ellie held her hand up to stop Danis talking, her face slowly relaxing into a soft smile. "It's okay, Danis.

I've just been so worried about Bastian, I failed to consider how hard this would be for you, too. So… how about you share everything you've been discussing?"

Jayce's anger returned as he watched the devastation on Ellie's face as she learned about Bastian's new problems. He couldn't believe the Stars' blatant, ongoing cruelty and disregard for the welfare of those who'd done everything they'd been asked. Why would they continue to punish Bastian when he'd already willingly sacrificed so much?

He saw the evidence of what he was feeling on Ellie's face and knew he needed to somehow diffuse the situation. Ellie on a rant against the Stars would not be good.

Sliding an arm around Ellie and pulling her closer, he formulated the words needed to pull them all away from the edge of the emotional deluge they were all so close to being consumed by. "Well, now that we're all up to speed, I think one thing has become blatantly obvious. Bastian is drowning from everything he's endured and continues to endure, so what he needs is our support and understanding. Ellie and I need to let go of the guilt we're feeling over what he's sacrificed for us, because seeing it only makes Bastian feel worse. Instead, we all need to focus on the positive outcomes from what he did and celebrate the wins not the losses. Would you all agree?"

Bella smiled at him with tears in her eyes. "Jayce

Raythawn, you are what the worlds have long been missing in their leadership roles. I have been around for a very long time, and never have I heard the selfless consideration for others you display. Well, except for that shown by Danis and Bastian when they chose to help you and your babies. Maybe there is hope for the future with leaders such as you."

Jayce was speechless after Bella's inspiring words. He'd never thought of himself as anything special, but when he thought about the atrocities committed by previous leaders, he realised that Bella was right. Power often led to greed for both possessions and more power. Selflessness had never been considered something a leader should possess. Until now!

Ellie

ELLIE HAD NEVER BEEN prouder of Jayce than she was at that moment. Of course, *she'd* been the beneficiary of Jayce's selflessness since the day they met. And she was ashamed to realise that her own selfishness, though unintentional, had only made Bastian's pain worse. How could she have failed to see what her own grief was doing to the poor boy? She'd been so wrapped up in her desire to repay Bastian for what he'd done that she hadn't seen how her constant displays of guilt and melancholic gratitude had only added to the burden the poor young prince carried.

"Oh Stars, Jayce. I feel terrible. I've been so consumed by how this was affecting—"

Jayce was surprised when Danis stepped in front of Ellie and took one of her hands in his, making Ellie pause mid-sentence. "Please don't beat yourself up over this Ellie. What you've been through demanded a certain degree of selfishness in order for you and the babies to survive. So, rather than focusing on your regret for what you did or didn't do, I truly believe that Bastian would prefer you to be happy and excited about the future. That is the best way to show him your gratitude."

"Wow," Ellie said, fighting back her own tears. "I want some of whatever you three have been ingesting. Seriously, I'm jealous. Your words are all so wise and eloquent, and I just blurt everything out with a total disregard for how it sounds or who it hurts."

Jayce chuckled, and she nudged him in the stomach. "Hey, like Danis said, stop beating yourself up. The worlds need people like you just as much as those like us. You, my darling, are a woman of action more than words, and we all love you just the way you are."

Well, damn. Now she felt like an idiot. She reached over and rubbed where she'd poked Jayce, a sheepish grin on her face. "Sorry, babe. Some old habits die hard."

"All good, sweetheart," Jayce whispered in her ear, before pulling away and kissing the top of her head. "Okay, so now that's all sorted, where do we go from here? I'm a bit worried Bastian won't be happy to find out we've been discussing him without him here. Any suggestions for how we let him down gently?"

Danis groaned. "Seeing I'm the one who introduced the detour to our original plan, I should probably be the one he takes his… whatever, out on. I'll leave a note in his room telling him I'm in the room next to his and that we need to talk when he wakes up. Then, depending on how he reacts, we'll go from there. Mum… what are your plans?"

Bella looked at them all, then sighed. "I'll need to get back to the Fae Realm tonight. Your father is covering for me in case anyone comes looking. But if Bastian agrees to trying the spells, I'll need a way to contact you and arrange a time."

Ellie grinned and began to unclasp her bracelet from her wrist. "I know this is weird, but Jayce and I have a telepathic link thanks to our bond, *except* when we are in different realms. So I came up with this idea to let Jayce know if I need him. Just keep it on you at all times, and if it disappears, we need you to come."

Bella's laugh was like a tinkling of bells. "See? Who needs eloquence when you have a brain like yours? What an ingenious way to circumvent a flaw in the magic. I have a feeling that you and I are going to become very good friends."

Ellie smiled and blushed, surprised by the warm tingle of contentment in her belly. "I'd love that, Bella. As soon as we've dealt with this latest catastrophe, it's a date."

Bella reached for the bracelet and put it in her pocket, then kissed Danis on the forehead, waved goodbye and was gone.

"Wow Danis. Your mum is awesome. I have a funny feeling she and my mother will get on like a house on fire," Ellie said, still staring at the spot where Bella had been.

"Yep. She's special alright. And my dad is the same. They sort of semi-adopted Bastian when we were little because the King and Queen… well let's just say they lack warmth."

Ellie's heart clenched at hearing about Bastian's home-life. She was so glad he had the love of the Farsight family growing up. Having Bella's influence in his life certainly explained how he had grown into such an amazing young man.

"Well, if you don't mind showing me the way to my room, I think it might be time for this day to be over," Danis said, looking as exhausted as she felt. "I can't say I'm looking forward to entering the dragon's den in the morning."

CHAPTER THIRTY-SEVEN

Bastian

Bastian opened his eyes and froze at the sight of his unfamiliar surroundings. *Where the Fates was he?* It wasn't until he spotted the pile of filthy clothing sitting on the floor that everything came flooding back. He closed his eyes again and pushed down the overwhelming urge to scream. What would be the point? It wouldn't change anything.

Throwing back the covers, he climbed out of bed and headed to the bathroom. A note was stuck to the outside of the bathroom door, and he instantly recognised Danis' messy scrawl. Damn, he hadn't had a chance to tell Danis he'd changed his mind and didn't want to lump his problems on Jayce and Ellie. The note was simple.

I'm next door. Just come over after you've read this. D.

Opening the door to the bathroom Bastian spotted a waste basket under the vanity. He screwed up the note and tossed it in. Then he relieved himself and stepped into the shower, moaning with pleasure at the feel of the hot, clean water washing away all evidence of his previous trials. He just wished it could be that easy to wash away the memories. *Nope. No escaping that reality.*

As soon as he stepped out of the shower, he realised he had a problem. He shuddered at the thought of wearing the filthy clothing currently sitting on the bedroom floor, but he wasn't aware of any other option. Maybe he'd just stay naked and climb back into bed. He couldn't really think of a good reason to stay up anyway.

Wrapped only in a towel, he was about to drop it and climb back into bed when he spotted the clothes sitting on the bedside table. What the hell? They hadn't been there when he went into the bathroom, so who—"

"Give me a yell when you're dressed and I'll be over," Danis voice came from the other side of the wall, answering his question for him.

He didn't answer, just pulled on the boxers, sweat-pants and T-shirt without even looking at them. No one would care what he looked like, so why should he? He looked into the mirror on the wall above the bedside table and froze. It wouldn't matter what he was wearing, he looked like something the cat dragged in. He hardly recognised the person looking back at him. His pale unshaven face and wild hair framed eyes filled with misery and defeat.

"Hey Bas, I didn't know if you heard—"

Danis sucked in a breath as Bastian turned to face him. Great, now he could add Danis to the list of people who felt sorry for him. He really needed to get his shit together and at least try to look normal.

"Shit man, you look terrible. So I don't suppose now is a good time to tell you I have some news?" Even in his morose state, Bastian could see that Danis looked really nervous about something. News? What kind of news could he possibly have learned between now and last night? Especially anything relevant to Bastian. Unless… no, Danis was his best friend. He wouldn't have spoken to anyone else about what Bastian considered his own private business.

"Da-nis. What the Fates have you done?" Bastian growled, the emotions he'd thought dead rising to the surface.

"Bas… I didn't know what else to do. You looked so… broken, and I had no idea where to even start to try and fix you. But when I told Jayce—"

Bastian's hands were clenched into fists, feelings of betrayal, helplessness and embarrassment raging through his body. "You went to Jayce without even asking me first? I can't believe you did this. I'd decided not to burden anyone else with my problems, and you go and blurt it to the world. Wait… does Ellie know?"

Bastian knew the answer without Danis even opening his mouth. Before he even knew what he was doing, Bastian had grabbed Danis by his shirt front and punched him in the face. He froze at the look of shock and then acceptance on Danis' face. There were no recriminations, no anger, just acceptance and regret.

Horrified by his actions, Bastian backed away from Danis, his eyes glued to the bruise already developing on Danis' jaw. "Shit Dan, I am so sorry. It's just… I don't…" And then to his absolute horror, he slumped to the floor and broke into huge wracking sobs.

Danis, the friend he'd just hit for trying to help him, sat on the floor beside him and threw an arm around his shoulder. "Hey man, I don't blame you for lashing out. I'd probably have done the same thing in your shoes. You need to just let it all out and then we can start trying to fix things."

"Wh-what's the p-point of anything anymore, Danis. It's all gone… everything—" he spluttered as he tried to rein in the sobs. His heart—*yes, the damned annoying organ was still there*—felt dead in his chest.

"Maybe not. Look, I don't want to get your hopes up too soon, but I *do* have some good news," Danis said, moving away to give Bastian some room to breathe. "Mum reckons—"

Bastian had been sucking in deep breaths and releasing them slowly, finally getting his emotions back under control. He almost choked on Danis' words. "Wait… what? When did you speak to your mother? Fates, is there anyone who doesn't know I have no magic?"

Then, to Bastian's utter astonishment, Danis burst out laughing. Okay, so maybe the whole situation had become so ridiculous it was funny. Before he knew it, Bastian was laughing just as hard as his friend. Damn, it felt good to laugh. Even if it was bordering on hysteria, it still beat sobbing.

"Well," Danis spluttered. "I did consider getting one of those sign-writers they use on Earth, but…"

Bastian just continued to laugh at Danis' absurd words, until they both lay on their backs holding their aching stomachs and breathing hard. "Thanks Dan…" Bastian said softly.

"That's what friends are for… remember?" Danis said, pushing against Bastian's shoulder.

"Yeah, but that was above and beyond—" Bastian froze at the knock on the door. He looked at Danis with a worried frown, but Danis just mouthed *trust me* and then called out to whoever was there to come in.

"Wow. What'd we miss?" Jayce asked as he entered the room, his eyes studying Bastian and Danis where they still lay on the floor.

"Good morning," Ellie said, following Jayce into the room. "Did we interrupt anything important?"

Danis sat up and rubbed the back of his neck.

"Nope. We were just considering going in search of coffee and some breakfast."

"Yeah… what he said," Bastian said, sitting up and attempting to pull himself together.

"So can I assume a conversation preceded… this?" Jayce asked, sweeping his hand out in front of him to indicate the floor.

"Well, we may have got sidetracked before Bastian found out my news. Maybe we could all sit and talk about it over breakfast?" Danis said, rubbing his jaw.

"Sounds like an excellent plan," Ellie said with a cheeky grin just before there was another knock at the door. "Lucky I ordered coffee and full breakfasts for four to be delivered before we came to visit."

Jayce

JAYCE WATCHED Bastian's face carefully as Danis told him about the conversation they'd had the previous evening. He hadn't missed the bruise developing on Danis' jaw, but it seemed the boys had sorted everything out before he and Ellie had arrived.

Jayce had also noticed that the defeat so evident in Bastian's eyes at dinner the previous night was slowly being replaced by a hint of hope and longing as he took in what Danis was saying. It felt good to know that they could help this boy who had done so much for Jayce and his family.

"So Bella is sure the Oracle would have told me if this loss of magic was part of the sacrifice?" Bastian asked Danis.

"Yep. She said there's no way this should have happened on top of losing the bond to your fated mate. So she's happy to try some spells she knows that might speed up the restoration of your magic, if you want," Danis replied, the relief at Bastian's improved emotional state evident.

"Fates, that would be awesome. I'm happy to try anything that might help. But how do we let Bella know we need her?"

Ellie chuckled and explained about the bracelet and how she only had to fetch it, and Bella would come. "So whenever you're ready, we can make it happen."

Bastian looked around, and whatever he saw made his face fall. "I can't believe I overreacted so badly. It was just such a shock, and on top of—"

Ellie pulled him into her arms and hugged him, tears running down her face. "Don't you dare beat yourself up for the way you reacted. You are one of the most selfless people I've ever met, and we will always be proud to consider you family."

Jayce patted Bastian on the shoulder and sighed. "Besides, if we ever want to reunite the realms as required by the prophecy, having your magic and your link to the throne restored is kind of important."

Danis cleared his throat, as always his voice of reason pulling them all back from the brink of emotional overload. "So, I'm thinking we should eat breakfast, fetch the bracelet and go from there?"

Jayce threw Danis a grateful smile and sat down at the small table covered in breakfast dishes, quickly followed by the others. They were soon all eating and discussing the immediate future, with Jayce offering to take Bastian and Danis to work with him so they could learn about the Witch and Dragon Realms. For now, at least, things were finally beginning to improve.

CHAPTER THIRTY-EIGHT

Ellie

It had been just over two weeks since they'd returned from Brevis, and life at Raythawn Castle had settled back into a reasonably comfortable routine. Jayce, Bastian and Danis spent most days at the Dragon Council, and Jayce had even invited Helena, the head of the Witch Council, to a meeting to discuss ideas about how to best approach the reconciliation between the realms.

And Ellie? Yeah, she had spent the entire two weeks trying not to get frustrated by the increasing size of her belly. But with ten weeks still to go, she'd resigned herself to the fact that not a lot would be achieved during that time.

She'd woken that morning with some cramping that felt like a mild version of her bad-feeling, but nothing to worry about. What had the doctor at the ultrasound called it? Oh yeah, Braxton Hicks. But after spending the morning alone in her room reading, she decided that the cramping had definitely become worse over the past few hours.

Of course her mother was in the Witch Realm, Iridia was spending the day with a friend, and Jayce and the boys were at work. The last thing she wanted to do was cause anyone to panic, and she knew that Jayce often shut down their communication when he was at work. Okay, so maybe she might be in trouble if anything was happening.

She'd just managed to convince herself that everything was fine when she looked down to find her hands doing the whole glowing thing again. Great, what the hell did that mean? Well, whatever it was, it was time to call Jayce home. She tried to message him, only to find his mind locked down tight. Shit… now what?

She started to giggle as a thought entered her mind. She focused on the shirt Jayce had been wearing when he left home that morning and fetched it with a flick of her wrist. Instantly, she wrapped the warm shirt covered in his scent around her and prayed her magic would behave until he got home.

Danis, Bastian and a very shirtless Jayce arrived in the lounge room in less than a minute. "Elle? Why the hell would you—"

Ellie said nothing as he stormed into the room, just held up her glowing—and now very much shaking—

hands and shrugged. She heard Bastian and Danis' gasps as Jayce crossed the room and lifted her into his arms.

"Where's your mother? Why didn't you call her?"

"Witch Realm," Ellie answered, groaning as another cramp started. "She said she'd be at her house if we needed her."

"What else is going on? Has your magic done anything weird like last time?"

"Nope. Just the glowing hands, unless you count the fact that what I thought were Braxton Hicks have been getting more painful and lasting longer every hour."

"Stars almighty Elle… you're in labour? But it's too early. The babies—"

"Will come when they're good and ready, Jayce. And it looks like that may be sooner than we'd expected. We should know better than anyone that what's considered normal doesn't ever apply to our family. So, would you mind popping over to the Witch Realm and bringing Mum back?" Ellie could feel the alien magic she'd felt once before swirling through her body. She needed her mother here to tell her everything was fine. Because it was… wasn't it?

Jayce looked torn between *his* need to hold her and *her* need for her mum. The man was seriously asking for an arse-kicking. "Jayce. I need you to put me down and get Mum. *Now... please...*" she practically growled.

Danis had moved closer and put his hand on Jayce's shoulder. "Jayce, she'll be fine. Bastian and I are both here, and we won't let anything happen to her. Now go, man, before you're rendered incapable of fathering any more children."

Ellie breathed a sigh of relief as Jayce finally placed her back on the lounge chair. "Don't move. I'll be right back," he whispered into her ear before kissing her on the forehead and disappearing.

"Seriously?" Ellie shouted into the now-empty spot in front of her. "Don't move? Where does he think I'm gonna go, and how would I even do it?"

She could see Bastian and Danis trying not to laugh and instantly felt better. She needed some humour in her life right about then. "Yeah, I don't think Jayce was in full control of his faculties when he left," Bastian said, and all three of them burst out laughing. Until Ellie's hands began to do the pulsing as well as glowing thing again.

"Okay, boys. I think you might need to put a bit more space between us for a minute. The last time this happened, my magic went for a little drive on autopilot," Ellie said, trying not to let the panic rising up inside her show. The boys looked at each other, shrugged and began to back up. She got the feeling they might have remembered hearing about her previous episode and didn't have a clue what to do.

"Ellie?" Relief flooded through her at the sound of her mother's voice. "What in all the realms is going on?" Ellie was so glad to see her mother she wanted to cry. But something told her now wasn't the time.

Besides, Jayce had arrived within seconds of her mum and he looked way too close to losing it. Having to leave her had obviously weighed heavily on his conscience.

"Jayce?" Her mum asked quietly. "Is this what was happening before her magic went haywire last time?"

Jayce nodded and tried to move toward Ellie, but her mum put her hand on his chest. "Wait… we need to see what Ellie wants us to do."

Ellie wanted to scream and cry that she wanted someone to hold her, but she knew she needed to let this rogue magic thing out first. "You need to all stay away. The last thing I want is for any of you to get hurt by what happens next… whatever that might be."

Ellie closed her eyes and tried to centre herself. Unlike last time, she knew the babies were coming, and she had no idea what to expect when it came to their magic. Ellie was pretty sure they didn't either. But if they were all going to survive this birth, she needed to get them to at least calm down and control their magic.

Hey, beautiful girls. Are you trying to tell me you're ready to come out and meet everyone? Because if you are, I need you to pull your magic back inside you until we can find out how it works. I'm worried that someone might get hurt if you let it just run wild. There'll be plenty of time for that once you're out. I know your Grandma Yvette is busting to teach you all about it.

Ellie sighed in relief as the pulsing in her hands stopped, and the glow faded away into nothing. Even the weird magic swirling in her belly started to recede, and Ellie wanted to jump for joy. "Yesss. You are such clever babies. *Now* we can have Daddy hold us while Grandma helps to make your entry into this world as easy as she can."

Bastian

Bastian felt as if he'd been pacing the lounge room forever. Jayce had moved Ellie to their bedroom once the magic had settled down, and he and Danis had been patiently waiting for news. Okay, so maybe *patiently* wasn't exactly the right word. More like worried and praying to the Fates that everything would be fine.

Well, everything to do with the birth of the twins that was. In the two weeks since they'd returned from Brevis, Bella had visited three times, and none of the spells she'd used seemed to have any effect on restoring his magic. She'd also reported on her last visit a few days ago that the King was getting more displeased by Bastian's absence from Court every day. But he was trying not to dwell on that today.

"C'mon Bas, stop stressing," Danis said from where he lounged back reading a book. "Do you really think a little thing like childbirth will be an issue for our amazing Ellie. She'll probably just—"

A loud baby's wail from upstairs told him that at least one of the babies was fine. Bastian was smiling for the first time all day as he slumped down onto the lounge. It wasn't long before a second wail joined the first, which was when he'd started to laugh. He hadn't said anything to anyone, but he'd been terrified there'd be something wrong with the babies after all they'd endured.

He laughed even harder when *Mr Cool-Calm-and-Collected* jumped up and fist pumped the air. "Woohoo… guess that makes us pseudo Uncles, eh?" Danis said as Bastian jumped back up and they hugged, both crying tears of joy at the final evidence that their quest had been successful. Not ten minutes later, Bastian sat looking longingly up the stairs when Jayce appeared there. Stunned at the elation radiating from every pore of the dragon shifter's body, he just continued to sit and stare.

"And here I thought you'd be busting to come and see my girls. Oh well, you're welcome to come up whenever you're ready," Jayce said, and turned to head back to his girls.

Bastian instantly snapped out of his stupor and raced to the stairs, laughing as Danis jostled him to try to be first. Damn, it had been a long time since he'd felt anything like the light-heartedness racing through his body. Who knew eh? Maybe these new lives could finally help to eradicate the darkness from his soul.

Standing in the doorway to Ellie and Jayce's room, Bastian took in the picture of their family basked in contented joy. This was what he'd given up so much to achieve, and he knew he'd do it all over again just to see this outcome. Jayce sat on the bed next to Ellie holding one of the girls, while Ellie held the other. As if a magnet were pulling at his stomach, he crossed the room and reached for a single hand of each of the bundles of perfection. "Welcome to the worlds, little ones."

Bastian stiffened as a surge of energy seemed to emerge from the twins' fingertips and race up his arms. He looked to Ellie in confusion, only to find tears rolling down her beautiful face. "The girls wanted to thank you for lending them your magic. Now, they're giving it back."

Bastian's heart squeezed as the huge empty void he'd felt since losing his magic and ties to the Spring Court was slowly starting to fill up. The twins' energy could fill every hole except the small one where the mate bond had been. Its absence would remind him every day of what he'd lost, but also what he'd gained.

This was what the Priestess and the Oracle had been referring to when they'd said the rewards would far outweigh the sacrifice. He would be able to watch this beautiful family thrive and enjoy their lives together, even if it was only from a distance. He may have lost his fated mate, but he'd gained the family he'd longed for his entire life.

Bastian

Bastian and Danis stood watching the small children playing together, unable to hold back their beaming smiles, a permanent fixture since they'd arrived at Raythawn Castle for the twins' fifth birthday. Bastian had been amazed to learn there was a significant time difference between the Dragon and Fae Realms, something they'd only become aware of since he'd started to spend more time visiting the Dragon Realm. Apparently, one day in the Fae Realm was two days in the Dragon Realm. Which didn't seem like much, until you watched two beautiful baby girls age at twice the rate of a Fae child.

So while the girls had turned five that day, it had only been two and a half years in Bastian's life since the incredible day they were born. He was sad that he didn't get to spend as much time as he would have liked with his new family, but his father, the King, had been ailing for the past year, and Bastian had been required to take up more and more of his duties. Still, it kept him busy and gave him less time to dwell on what he would always consider his... loss.

One thing he always made time for was to read everything he could find on the fated mate bond. It hadn't taken him long to discover that there were no previous records of the way his mate bond had been broken. Bastian had embraced this news with both hands, hoping it meant another fated mate bond was possible for both of them in the future.

The Oracle's words when he'd agreed to the sacrifice demanded by the Fates and Stars often played in his head.

Both fate and destiny are susceptible to changes caused by the choices we make and the courage we show in the face of adversity. You must always embrace any opportunity to change what is.

So that's what he did. Every day, he woke and prayed it would be the day that would present the opportunity for that change. Because, unlike most who felt nothing until they met their fated mate, he knew what he was missing and refused to believe he would have to spend his entire life without ever feeling it again.

A tugging on his pants leg drew his attention down to the adorable child in front of him. He knew it was

Sera by the single streak of silver running through the copper-gold hair, exactly like her mother's.

Bastian instantly squatted down so they were on eye level. "And what can I do for you, young lady?" he asked softly.

Sera reached for his hand and looked him directly in the eyes. "Could you please... ummm... push me on the swing?"

"I would be honoured to perform such a pleasant duty," Bastian replied, and Sera giggled. "Please, just lead the way, and I will follow."

He stood up and turned to Danis to tell him where he'd be and almost burst out laughing at the scene unfolding behind him.

"So I guess that means I'm stuck with you," Angel was saying, her arms folded as she scowled up at Danis.

Danis adopted the exact same scowl on his face before replying. "Excuse me, young lady. I don't think either of your parents would be very happy to see and hear this behaviour from one of their daughters."

"What? So now you're gonna run crying to Mummy and Daddy cos I didn't suck up like Sera did?" Angel's scowl had deepened, and Bastian couldn't help thinking how *un-angel-like* she was behaving.

"Well, how about we make a deal. You ask me nicely to push you on the swing, and we'll forget this conversation ever happened," Danis said, trying to hide his smirk.

Angel appeared to be pondering her choices, before

she finally shrugged. "Fine. It's a deal." Then the scowl was replaced by a dazzling smile. "Danis, could you please push me on the swing." Her voice was sugary sweet, and Bastian didn't know how Danis managed to hold back his laughter.

"Your wish is my command, fair maiden," Danis said with a formal bow.

"Whatever," Angel said, grabbing Danis' hand and beginning to drag him behind her. Bastian didn't miss the way she had to choke back her giggle. "But if we don't go now, we'll never even get a turn. And I'll have wasted my time with all this stupid talking stuff."

That was the final straw. Bastian and Danis both burst out laughing as they were dragged toward the waiting swings.

END OF BOOK THREE

FROM JENNIFER

Thank you so much for reading Book 3 in the Morwitch Series. I hope you enjoyed reading it as much as I did writing it. Originally, this series was written as a duology, but Jayce and Ellie really wanted me to continue their story. Stay tuned for more drama when the twins celebrate their 18th birthday.

You can visit my website for further updates and release dates, as well as subscribe to my newsletter at:

jenniferredmile.com

I WOULD BE FOREVER GRATEFUL IF YOU WOULD CONSIDER LEAVING A REVIEW ON AMAZON.